THE BUTTERFLY

RYAN BLUMENTHAL

New Generation Publishing

CONTENTS

CHAPTER 1:

THE BUTTERFLY

Deep within the impenetrable forests of Central Eastern Africa there rests a mountain range covered in thick clouds and mists. From these majestic mountains flow forest streams, which merge to form pools and rivulets, which once again, merge and flow, to form mighty waterfalls containing some of the purest waters known to man.

The stones of the streams are wet and black and the streams in the forests flow fresh and the waters bubble clear.

Within one of these impenetrable forest pools, a singular caterpillar crawls awkwardly upon a leaf. This little luminescent green-red-and-blue caterpillar crawls quite fearlessly upon its leaf, for it contains a poison so deadly it could easily kill an elephant! The poison is obtained from the particular tree upon which the young worms feed. And as the caterpillar grows, so its poison concentrates and intensifies. When this little caterpillar eventually turns into a butterfly, the poison concentrations are at its most intense.

Some say that this poison is so fierce that it may even be absorbed through the intact skin of its victim. Locals who have seen the powerful toxicity of this little worm believe it to be one of the most toxic poisons on earth!

The beauty of the butterfly is also unparalleled. Its majestic colours could hypnotize even the most unobservant of onlookers. Its wings erupt violently in the most brilliant primary colours, all meticulously arranged in a swirl and a whirl next to one another! Each of the extreme primary colours neatly arranged next to one another. It was almost as if the Creator created this butterfly out of pure folly! And when this little butterfly flew, it had an awkward yet confident way about it.

How and why this particular species evolved to contain such a deadly poison was unknown to the local villagers, for it had no natural enemies. Why the Creator would put such a poisonous species on this earth was an even greater mystery!

CHAPTER 2:

THE BIRD

What the young herdsboy had seen had completely astonished him. He could not believe his own eyes!

He was simply washing in the river when he observed what happened. He saw a bird try and catch an insect.

As the bird caught the insect – it dropped suddenly out of the sky and fell into the water. Dead!

The herdsboy watched with fascination as the bird floated lifelessly on the surface of the water. Eventually it floated to exactly the same spot where he was washing. Surely the bird must have been old or sick for it to have died so swiftly?

Being a curious and a cautious herdsboy, he carefully decided to take a closer look at the bird. At first he took a stick and prodded the bird. There were no injuries noted externally on its feathers or body.

He then took the lifeless bird in both hands and carefully placed it on the river bank. He carefully opened its beak and saw a brilliantly coloured butterfly lodged within its upper throat.

'*Uvemvane !*' He said under his breath, as he saw the butterfly. He had heard stories about these poisonous butterflies from the elders as a child.

Suddenly, one of the butterfly wings twitched and fluttered ever so lightly against his hand.

He carefully examined the bird again and then focussed on the butterfly. There was nothing else abnormal to be found.

He went back down to the river to wash his hands. His right hand began to itch.

As he reached the water he suddenly became light-headed. Within a short space of time he became dizzy, nauseous and suddenly felt very weak. Even before he could wash his hands, he collapsed face down into the water. His body didn't even shake or twitch.

What had so swiftly killed the bird had now also killed him.

CHAPTER 3:

THE DISCOVERY

The herdsboy's lifeless body was discovered by the elderly women of his village later that afternoon. They themselves had gone down to the river to wash. The women didn't get too close to the body, nor did they touch the body. All they did was simply identify the body as that of the young herdsboy.

The elderly men were called to investigate the scene and much animation followed.

One of the elderly men went closer to the body and touched it with his large walking stick. He turned the body over and confirmed it to be that of their young herdsboy.

The old man was completely without an explanation. He saw the lifeless body of the young man lying face down in the water. Nearby, on the river bank was a freshly-dead-bird. There were no injuries on the body of the herdsboy. There were no footprints of wild and/or dangerous animals in the sand. The sky was clear and there was no obvious reason for his death.

The old man of the village looked up towards the sky. His eyes were clouded with age and his mouth was almost without teeth. He breathed in deeply through his nostrils. The frown remained on his leathery, weather-beaten forehead.

The old man further examined the scene of death. A little downwind, hidden from general view, he found the dead remains of the brilliantly coloured butterfly.

'Uvemvane!' He exclaimed, with absolute conviction, as he pointed to the butterfly with his arthritic finger.

The villagers had seen this kind of thing before; they all knew of the dangers of this little butterfly and they were satisfied with the conclusion of their investigation. Why this herdsboy touched this butterfly was unknown to them all. From childhood all the villagers clearly understood the dangers of this little butterfly.

The tribe knew not to touch the body. They knew how fierce the toxin of the butterfly was. And so they left the mortal remains of the herdsboy lying alone on the river bank. They didn't even try and bury the body.

Over the weeks to come, no flies would descend upon the body. No vultures, hyenas or even jackals would scavenge upon the body.

The body of the bird and the butterfly were also left untouched, left to nature to decompose by themselves.

The story of the herdsboy and the butterfly would, with time, become just another of Africa's many long-forgotten tragedies.

CHAPTER 4:

FROM PEACE TO WAR

Life continued at a relatively relaxed pace in the small African village. The women worked hard, the children played hard and the men seemed to not do much at all – as was the normal rhythm in Africa.

However peace does not last forever. During the high moon, some seemingly nomadic thieves had entered their small village and had stolen some of the villager's maize and cattle!

Despite the best efforts to track the footprints of the thieves, the thieves were too clever and they seemed to have vanished into thin air.

The elders decided to hold a meeting under the large baobab tree in the centre of the village the following day. They needed to discuss the theft. There was some concern, frowns were present on their faces and much worry hung in the air.

'What are we going to do about the theft?' asked one of the villagers.

'Our supplies are nearly finished' exclaimed another.

There was much talk under the big tree that day and the African sun burned fiercely through the sky.

One of the elders suggested they build better barriers which would hopefully deter the thieves.

The villagers decided that this was an excellent idea and they helped collect fever-tree thorn branches. This large tree had large thorns and was much revered in the region for its defensive properties. The villagers used the branches to reinforce their precious cattle and to protect their precious supply of maize.

A few days later the thieves attacked again! This time they had set fire to the dried-out fever tree branches and had stolen a few more cattle and the last of the maize!

The villagers were so busy trying to fight the fire and protect their huts that the thieves managed to escape once again and they disappeared into the blackness of the night!

The elders decided to call another very important meeting under the baobab tree the next morning.

Obviously, the situation was very tense and the entire village was under threat. The fire of the previous night had nearly injured some of the villagers. And what was more, their precious cattle and maize had, once again, been stolen!

The situation was so worrisome that, the elders decided to place armed guards on duty at night to protect the last of their livestock.

All was peaceful in the village for the next few weeks, until the next high-moon when the thieves struck again! This time they struck much harder and much fiercer than before! They had assaulted the guards on duty and had stolen the last of their remaining cattle. The situation was now very desperate! The elders knew that their once-peaceful village was suddenly under very real threat.

CHAPTER 5:

THE DECISION UNDER THE BAOBAB TREE

The villagers were still shocked at the sheer ruthlessness and brutality of the attack. The thieves had stolen everything in the village stores! There was now suddenly no more maize and no more cattle.

The tension could be felt in the air. Luckily the women could still fish in the nearby streams. And luckily there were still some fruits, seeds and berries to be found in the nearby forests. And there was also always the opportunity of finding some bush meat. Although, having said all this, bush meat was becoming quite scarce in recent months. The villagers were generally depressed and angry about the theft.

Just when things seemed to be at their worst, the thieves struck again! Once again they attacked at night, in the dark, in the middle of the night, while everyone was sleeping. This time they kidnapped three of the young womenfolk from the village. When the men from the village tried to chase the thieves, they were so weak from lack of food that they could not catch them!

One of the villagers managed to come close to the thieves and he was viciously attacked.

The village had lost all their cattle, they had lost all their maize and now they had lost three of their young womenfolk! The villagers were feeling very desperate and their mood was at an all-time low. The only thing keeping them motivated was anger. Anger and revenge!

The elders decided to once again call an urgent meeting under the baobab tree.

The villagers of the small tribe knew of no other village in the vicinity, and the presence of thieves was quite surprising to them all. Where had these thieves come from? Who were these people? How many of them were there? And most importantly, were their womenfolk unharmed?

The solution seemed to arrive by itself, almost spontaneously. Making the connection did however require a certain amount of daring. Whereas in the past such a solution may have seemed somewhat unreasonable for such a peace-loving village, it now seemed perfectly reasonable!

No one individual had a greater reputation than any of the others in the village. Every member had an equal chance to speak. No villager was more articulate or had a distinctly commanding personality than any of the others. No villager took over the meeting and reduced the rest to passive and obedient bystanders. Everyone had a chance to speak and everyone's opinion was respected!

The meeting commenced with several of the villagers suggesting an offensive attack. There was much approval of this suggestion and all nodded in agreement. And then, as if from nowhere, the idea of using the caterpillar / butterfly poison seemed to come from the villagers all at once! *"Uvemvane!"* was the word which was uttered almost from nowhere. The death of the young herdsboy was still relatively fresh in their minds. It was almost as if they knew that this was a message from their ancestors. They would coat their arrow heads with this butterfly poison! They would hunt down the thieves, they would bring back their womenfolk, and they would bring back their cattle … And they would kill these thieves! A lone vulture soared high-above them. Certainly it could sense the smell of blood in the air!

CHAPTER 6:

THE WEAPONIZATION OF THE CATERPILLAR

There were two groups. One group consisted of womenfolk who went into the forest to find the specific caterpillars and / or the butterflies. The other group consisted of menfolk tasked with carving and designing the bows and arrows.

The womenfolk had some difficulty finding the caterpillars and the butterflies due to their rarity. However, after about a week of intense searching, the womenfolk had discovered at least three of these small caterpillars. There simply were no more caterpillars or butterflies to be found!

The men had carved fire-hardened acacia wood into spears and arrows.

Now the villagers had to coat the blood of the caterpillars on to the tips of the weapons. The villagers knew just how toxic these caterpillars were. Even the womenfolk were careful not to touch the little worms when collecting them!

The entire process demanded a completely hands-off approach! The caterpillars were ground up in a special mortar-and-pessel. The arrow tips were then dipped into the crushed and squashed caterpillar paste and the arrow-tips were left to dry in the sun.

The next day, the villagers decided to test the efficacy of their new weapon. It was agreed that someone should head out into the forest and try and shoot the biggest animal that he could find!

The biggest animal in this part of Africa was of course the elephant! Yet elephants were so scarce in this part of the world in recent months. In fact, no villager had even seen an elephant footprint in a long time.

The villagers decided to send Bo – short for Bonang. Bo was the cousin of the young herdsboy who died while washing in the river. Bo would be perfect to test the potency of the poison as he was quite adept with bow and arrow. He had a good reputation amongst the villagers as a relatively good hunter. He would walk stealthily through the forest until he came across a big enough animal. This was an excellent idea the village elders thought, and Bo agreed to this important mission.

Bo was in his late teens, yet he was very much mature for his age. A thin moustache was present on his upper lip. He wore a traditional string around his abdomen. Bo felt honoured to be involved in such an important mission. He would surely test how dangerous these arrows were!

He had been walking stealthily for a length of time through the forest and yet he had found nothing! There simply were no apes, antelopes or birds to be found! It was almost as if the animals knew they were being hunted, or perhaps the thieves had something to do with this, Bo mused to himself.

Bo came to the end of his home range. Beyond his tribal home range he knew not what lay beyond the thick and impenetrable forest. Some of the elders had walked further in the past, yet according to them it was just more thick and more impenetrable forest. According to the elders, the forest would slowly rise into the mountains, becoming covered within thick mists and even thicker clouds.

Despondent, he headed back to his village. He was tired and hungry. Tomorrow was another day, he thought. When he arrived back home however he discovered – to his utter, sheer and nauseating horror – that his entire village had been burned to the ground! All of the villagers lay dead and their corpses lay burning and ashen on the ground. All the children were dead. All the village elders were dead! The thieves had attacked again! This time they had massacred his entire village! Everyone he knew. Dead! And now, only he survived...

CHAPTER 7:

KING MAKOHANI

The King enjoyed his eagle hatchlings grilled over an open flame. These were of his favourite little delicacies.

These tiny, still-sizzling roasted birds – head, beak, and feet still attached, guts intact inside their plump little bellies. This was his rare and forbidden meal!

At the start of each new moon, his warriors would go out in search of these rare little eagle hatchlings. Typically they were to be found on precariously high mountain cliffs. The warriors would risk falling and attacks from the adult eagles, for if they returned empty-handed, they were to be tortured in front of the entire kingdom.

King Makohani was as ruthless and as savage as they come. On his birthday, he would typically mix his own excrement into milk and add an amount of killer-bee honey and make all the warriors of his kingdom drink of his "magic potion". He believed that it was this magic potion which imbued his men with supernatural powers.

Anyone who dared defy the King would simply be tortured or killed!

Traitors were made to stretch a freshly-dead animal hide between their teeth. Animal hides needed to be stretched and this agonizing process would take days to dry under the hot African sun. Traitors stood, wrists tied behind their backs, biting with clenched teeth and at the same time stretching the skins of the freshly dead animals.

If they were to weaken or drop the hides from their mouths, they would be beaten with sjamboks (a type of whip) and sometimes even killed outright.

Makohani's sentries would enforce Makohani's laws. His right hand man was Maphuti, who was in charge of enforcing his laws.

King Makohani ruled over much of Africa at the time. His Kingdom was over 10 000 strong! His kingdom was exceptional and mighty for its time and was feared by all. His warriors were likened to fierce army ants who would invade nearby villages. His warriors worked very cleverly and very stealthily.

He lived in what he called his 'vulture's nest' – high atop a mountain – overlooking his troops below. The architecture of his residence was ahead of its time, honed into the rock face – like a vulture's nest. Only he and his most senior sentries lived atop the mountain. They were able to view the entire kingdom from horizon to horizon. The foot path from the foothills below to his residence would take a fit man several hours to ascend!

Their *modus operandi* was revolutionary for its time: A small unit of his warriors would first find a nearby village. Then they would send in one or two *'thieves'* to steal the village's cattle and maize. This 'petty theft' approach would then escalate over the next few months. Then, when the villagers were weak, the 'thieves' would kidnap their women, descend *en-masse* upon the village and kill all the men and all the children of the village. The women would typically be used as wives for his warriors or as labourers. The children would be trained to become future warriors. This technique worked so well because the victims were weakened and unable to defend themselves at the time of conquest.

King Makohani was busy eating one of the grilled hatchlings when his senior sentry, Maphuti entered his hut. Makohani had waited for the sizzling flesh and fat to quieten down a bit. Then he grasped the bird gingerly by its hot skull and placed it feet-first into his mouth- only its grilled head and beak protruding. It was revolting to watch this man, struggling to swallow the unctuous mouthful of steamingly hot bird guts and bone bits.

'We have burned the entire village to the ground my King, we now have their women as our slaves. We also have a few of their children. ' Maphuti said with blunt arrogance.

The King crunched down into his small flame-roasted bird and its blood and juices trickled over his chin. One could hear the first snap of tiny bones as he bought his molars slowly downwards through the bird's ribcage with a wet crunch, Makohani was rewarded with a scalding hot rush of burning fat and guts down his throat. Those around him could hear the small bones of the roast eagle hatchling crackle and crunch in his mouth. One could almost imagine the thin bones, fat, meat, skin and organs compacting in- and on themselves.

Maphuti cast a nervous look at the other eleven sentries who sat around Makohani in the hut.

Makohani then slowly drew the head in and the beak with his tongue, which until now had been hanging from his lips, and he slowly crushed the skull. He wiped his mouth with his thick leathery hand and chewed very slowly, breathing through his nostrils, as he listened to this new information. One could see the delight in his dark eyes.

Makohani chewed and swallowed quite audibly. He wiped his mouth again and looked straight at Maphuti.

'Did you destroy all the men of the village? ' he asked.

'Yes, my King, all the men are dead.'

'Good! For even the smallest ember can start a fire!'

The King reached for his Calabash of killer-bee honey and milk – (this batch did not contain his own excrement). He guzzled the mixture, audibly gulping, as the rest drizzled down his chest.

The King looked at Maphuti with fierce, half-crazed eyes.

'You are welcome to the first choice of their women, now go!'

CHAPTER 8:

NEVER CUT DOWN A TREE IN THE WINTERTIME

Bo was in great shock. Everyone that he had ever known had been massacred and destroyed. The village's womenfolk seemed to have been captured and his entire village had been burned to the ground.

As with all matters of this nature, his first thoughts turned to rescuing his womenfolk and to revenge. But who was the enemy? How many of them were there? Why did the enemy want to attack his peaceful little village? Were his womenfolk still alive? What weapons did the enemy have at their disposal? How vulnerable was the enemy? The questions seemed to flow almost spontaneously.

Bo stood alone under the large baobab tree. He knew he had a powerful weapon at his disposal. *Even though he hadn't officially tested it yet* (because there were simply no animals to test it on), all he knew was that it was this poison which had killed his cousin.

It was an old saying of his village '*Never cut down a tree in the wintertime*'. Bo knew not to make decisions in low times. He knew never to make important decisions when his mood was low. He knew how important it was to wait. He knew how important it was to be patient. He knew that all storms pass.

Instinctively, he understood that he had to protect himself from the enemy. He had to go into hiding. He was currently insufficiently prepared to attack his enemy. He had to get information. He had to gather himself. He had to get mentally, emotionally and physically fit.

He knew that the caterpillar poison would be able to crush his enemy completely. But how close would he need to be to the enemy in order to deliver his arrow?

Surely the enemy would want to kill him in the process.

Bo understood that his womenfolk would be used and abused the longer he waited. Yet he made an important judgement call under that baobab tree. He understood that his womenfolk were already destroyed. His womenfolk were probably being raped and tortured as he thought these thoughts. As far as he was concerned, his captured womenfolk were already dead.

Bo would disappear – enough time for the enemy to completely forget about him –

During his time in exile, he would gather as much information on his enemy as possible. He would train his body and he would train his mind. He would learn to suppress his emotions. Ultimately, he would seek revenge upon his enemy and rain fire upon them.

And so, tragically, alone, with his singular bow and arrow, he disappeared like a ghost into the deep forests of Central-East Africa.

He realized that he had to try and see things through different eyes. He needed to try and understand what had just happened to him. He had stopped for some water in a stream when he thought he heard something. He had actually managed to hear one of the quietest sounds in nature – he had managed to hear the sound of a butterfly flapping its wings. In a strange way, this little moment helped focus Bo away from his pain and suffering. Pain is inevitable thought Bo – but suffering is not.

Bo watched the butterflies flying awkwardly amongst the trees. He realized that we are all going to experience physical and emotional pain as we grow older. We cannot stop the pain. Bo realized that it's how we react to this pain which is important. He had to try and turn this pain into good. Bo realized that he *had* to take revenge. It would be this 'spirit of revenge' which would define him and keep him going. All he knew was that he was not ready physically or emotionally to go into battle yet. He didn't have the energy or the discipline to kill his enemy. He needed time to heal. Bo felt tired.

And so he just walked and walked and walked until he knew he would have to stop and rest.

And the little butterflies continued to *'flutter by'*, all around him, while he walked. Flapping their little wings in the forest, they created the tiniest drafts of air, which created the tiniest little air currents, which created the tiniest little drafts of air. Nothing happens in Nature without consequence. Few men truly understand cause and effect. Could these tiny little drafts of air caused by the butterfly's wings ultimately affect the weather? Could such a seemingly insignificant event really have large-scale consequences? Could this have been the first stage of the thunderstorm which would ultimately unleash itself in months to come? Could these little insignificant wing beats be the cause of his ultimate death?

CHAPTER 9:

EXILE

Bo fled eastwards and then southwards. He travelled for many days. He drank when he got thirsty and hunted when he got hungry. In between he foraged on berries and leaves, but he generally had no appetite and his heart was very heavy. For the first time in his life he travelled beyond the boundaries of his known world. He crossed vast plains, savage rivers; climbed endless hills and seemed to walk forever and alone over the savannahs.

His mood was that of a stone sinking soundlessly in deep, deep water.

Many weeks after his village was destroyed and his fellow villagers were massacred, he arrived at a place which seemed almost comfortable enough for him to settle.

Bo wasn't tall and he wasn't short. When his fellow villagers were still alive, his job was simply to watch the cattle. He had come from a long line of cattle herders. His father was a cattle herder. And his grandfather was a cattle herder. Even his cousins were cattle herders. He was still relatively young, in his late teens, and his beard hadn't even begun to grow yet.

'*I will settle here for the time being because there is good water,*' Bo gazed towards the trickle of water oozing from a rocky wall, '*I will be safe here because I am high up and able to see all around me.*' Bo stood on his rocky outcrop – a lone hill completely surrounded by endless grasslands.

He could see herds of animals grazing in the distance. The giraffes seemed to stare and look in his general direction. Yet one of the giraffes was staring in another direction – a single giraffe was looking the other way! Bo knew that one should always follow the gaze of giraffe because they always stared at potentially dangerous things. When he followed the gaze of the other giraffe, he could see a lone human being walking in the distance! Who was this man walking alone in the middle of nowhere? Was Bo being followed? Was Bo being tracked? Bo became feverish with nervous excitement. He had to remain calm.

Bo could see that this was a strange man. It was no-one he knew from his village.

'I must catch him and interrogate him!' thought Bo.

And with that, he descended quickly and deeply into the valley and proceeded to hunt down his victim in the grasslands.

He moved quietly and with purpose, like a leopard stalking his prey.

'*I must keep him alive*', thought Bo.

'*I must find out who he is and what he knows*'...

CHAPTER 10:

THE MAN WITH THE RABBIT FOOT AROUND HIS NECK

The air was heavy and hot. There was no wind and the sky seemed to push down upon him.

A grey go-away bird let out a very slow and very deliberate *'go-awaaaaaay'*, which was the distress call of the bird. A more enthusiastic 'go-away' usually meant nothing; however a slow and deliberate *'go-awaaaaaaay'* meant, in the bird world, that there was danger!

The stranger heard the call of the bird and caught visual sight of Bo. The stranger immediately began to increase his pace and started running. Bo followed with his bow-and-arrow. He ran after the stranger. Until, the Stranger stopped dead in his tracks. Hands up. He surrendered.

'Stop!' Cried the Stranger, *'Please don't hurt me.'* The Stranger spoke the same language as Bo!

Bo could see that the stranger was somewhat older than him and wore a rabbit's foot around his neck. The stranger seemed to have no expression on his face. He was a man who had no emotion left to give. Bo could immediately see that this was a man who had been through a lot and had no more emotion left to give. There were also multiple criss-cross scars over his chest and back.

Bo ordered the stranger to get on his knees and bow his head.

The stranger obeyed. All the while Bo had his arrow tightly-pulled and the arrow tip was pointing at his face.

'Who are you? Where do you come from? Where are you going?' Bo asked, wondering if the stranger could understand him. He knew that these three questions were very powerful and that his tribe always used to ask these three questions to all strangers, including themselves!

'I have no name,' 'I do not know where I come from, and I do not know where I am going.' The man with the rabbit foot around his neck replied.

'LIAR!' screamed Bo.

And with that Bo tore off the stranger's worldly possession – the necklace containing the rabbit foot- The necklace snapped off the neck, the leather throng dangled from his left hand.

'This rabbit foot around your neck is not so lucky now!' mocked Bo as he came face-to-face with his captive .

'It wasn't lucky for the rabbit either!' responded the captured man.

Bo smiled, at hearing this. He walked boldly and courageously straight up to the Stranger and placed the arrow right close to his face. The arrow was pulled tightly on the bow and his fingers were clenched white, sweaty and ready to fire. The deadly tip of the arrow, laced with butterfly-blood, was but an eyelash away from the stranger's eye.

'Alright, I will tell you everything!' The stranger immediately broke down.

The captured man turned out to be a defector from the Kingdom of Makohani. He had no name, yet was known as the one with the rabbit foot around his neck. He didn't even put up a fight! There was no resistance. This lone refugee simply submitted. It looked like he had always been oppressed, for he submitted naturally. The stranger suddenly began to weep, tears began to fall from his eyes and he completely and utterly broke down.

The defector was as timid as a dog with its tail tight between its legs. One could see that he had been beaten and abused. He was completely submissive! He had multiple scars criss-crossing his entire body where he had been whipped in the past. What Bo had captured was a completely broken man.

The man appeared relatively intelligent. He had a hard, weathered face, it was impossible to tell how old he was. Clearly, though, he had had a hard life.

Apparently, he had fallen out of favour with the King, because he could not find any more Eagle Hatchling for the King to eat! King Makohani had viciously lost his temper and had ordered that the man be punished the following morning.

The punishment conceived by King Makohani was particularly sadistic. He had designed a torture and execution room made entirely of stone, mud and thatch hollow, with a door on one side and raised on stilts. The condemned person would be locked in the room until he succumbed.

Only by sheer luck did he manage to escape and was busy fleeing for his life when he was captured by Bo!

The man with the rabbit foot around his neck began telling story after story of just how evil King Makohani was. And once he started talking – he almost couldn't stop! Despite him being tired and almost dehydrated! Stories or rape, stories of murder and stories of mass genocide oozed from this stranger's parched lips! It transpired that the stranger's village was *also* burned to the ground in a very similar fashion to Bo's village! His entire tribe had *also* been systematically massacred, just like Bo's! His wife had been kidnapped. His children, his friends and his neighbours – Everyone he ever knew was killed by the Savage King Makohani!

The stranger wished for nothing more than Revenge!

"I want to chase him before me, I want to rob him of his wealth, I want to see his near and dear bathed in tears, I want to rob him of his cattle, and I want to sleep on the bellies of his wives and daughters!"

The man with the rabbit's foot around his neck was now sobbing and his forehead was on the sand.

Bo realized that King Makohani was a very dangerous enemy indeed!

'Get up!' ordered Bo. *'You are coming with me! What happened to your village also happened to my village! I too, am a survivor. It sounds to me that we have a common enemy.'*

Bo helped the man to his feet. He even helped dust him off.

'Where are we going?' asked the stranger.

'To that hilltop', pointed Bo.

And so the two of them began walking.

Bo realized that he had to suppress all human compassion and emotion. He realized that he would have to kill whoever stands in his way. This he knew lay at the heart of the art of the combat to come. He would have to vanquish his enemy completely!

CHAPTER 11:

MAKOHANI THE UNTOUCHABLE

Over the next few weeks, Bo was told more and more of this power-hungry and savage King who was guarded day and night by layer-upon-layer of his sentries.

His own men thought he was a military genius, yet in the same breath they all feared him for the sheer brutality of his reign.

Makohani's kingdom was fashioned after the Matebele ant colony, where he was Chief in Command. The ants' sophisticated raiding behaviour was mimicked by Makohani's fierce warriors who overwhelmed various other tribes during the time.

His laws were very simple and his kingdom appeared to work relatively well. His sentries would patrol day and night. If anyone caused any trouble, whatsoever, in any way or form – Makohani would call the parties into his massive thatched hut where he would decide their fate. The decision would obviously be based on his mood for that day. There was no logic or reason or process to explain how he came up with his punishments. Oftentimes, as was his way, he would simply have them work in slavery or have them dispatched in some or other dramatic way, often as a form of entertainment for the rest of the Kingdom.

Makohani had chosen a particularly gruesome revenge for one of his wives who denied him intercourse because she was sick at the time. He had locked her in a hut and placed two hyenas inside with her: they devoured her and, in the morning, Makohani burned the hut, with the hyaenas, to the ground. Stories such as these paralyzed all those around him. His methods were particularly cruel, sadistic and imaginative. He would always find the most dramatic way to send a message to his people.

Makohani's tribe grew larger and larger with every invasion of nearby villages. The men of the invaded villages would be killed and the women and children would be taken for his kingdom. The children were then taught to develop a "warrior"-type mind set. He would drill his troops frequently, forcing them to march barefoot, for extended distances a day, over hot, rocky terrain!

Boys and girls, aged-six, joined Makohani's forces as apprentice warriors and served as carriers of rations, supplies like cooking pots and sleeping mats, and extra weapons until they joined the main ranks at age-twelve. From the time they could stand they were initiated into his army... Taught never to retreat, never to surrender, taught to show no pain, no mercy and they were constantly tested.

Everyone feared King Makohani. Everyone wanted him dead. Everyone despised him! There had even been a few attempts on his life, yet somehow he always managed to survive. All those who attempted to assassinate him were now dead. He had established himself as the *de facto* Ruler of the land.

All those in his presence would tremble with fear and no-one even made eye contact with him.

Over the years many had tried to assassinate their power-hungry King.

One such assassination attempt happened on a late wintery afternoon. Makohani had created his very own warm-water mountain rock-pool high up in the overhanging cliffs named the 'Vultures Nest'. Maidens would carry warm pots of water from the fires in the village below upon their heads and walk up the steep pathway with the pots of steaming water on their heads.

Row-upon-row of women would labour-intensively and pour pot-by-pot of water into the rocky-pool until it was brimming full and steaming hot. King Makohani and his sentries would then arrive, and, closely-guarded, Makohani would bathe in the purified and steaming waters.

One of the women who had particular reason to hate the King, because he had killed her entire family and forced himself upon her, decided to assassinate him.

She had hidden behind one of the rocks with a make-shift knife. She had waited patiently for him to immerse himself in the steaming water. Makohani always believed that one should immediately immerse oneself in steaming water and never immerse oneself in a slow manner. His entire philosophy was to subject oneself quickly to pain and accept it. This was the philosophy which he had imbedded into the minds of all his warriors.

Makohani was busy immersing himself in the steaming water when the woman suddenly and unexpectedly lunged at him from behind, her make-shift knife held high, she stabbed him in the upper back! Makohani fell forward and the knife did not penetrate into his thoracic cavity, it seemed she had missed the intercostal space and the make-shift blade had deflected off his bony scapula!

Makohani, immediately rose from the water. He silently and fiercely stared deep into her soul. The silence of that stare could be heard for eternity. She was enraged and frustrated. He could smell her fear and he inhaled it deeply through his nostrils. He breathed her in. He silently gestured to his sentries. The woman's eyes were wide and full of fear for she knew that her fate had been sealed.

Makohani made himself very comfortable in his rock-pool, his large arms outstretched behind him, as he watched his sentries gang-rape the poor woman multiple times. He then asked for a drink, while he watched them extinguish the life out of her in the most slow and painful of ways.

Makohani then ordered that her body be impaled on a large wooden pole, high up on the overhanging cliffs, for all the Kingdom to see. He also needed to feed his vultures. His message was very clear.

Another failed assassination attempt happened several months later. This time it was one of his own sentries. While Makohani was sleeping, the massive sentry quietly stole into his hut. The sentry snuck into the large thatched structure that was Makohani's private residence. It was very dark and the entire village was quiet. Only the dim orange glow of dying fires seemed to create an eerie glow in the night.

As soon as the sentry had entered his sleeping chamber, an arrow from no-where perforated through-and-through the sentries' skull. Makohani had booby-trapped his very own sleeping chamber! The bow and arrow were pulled tight and the sentry had inadvertently tripped the wire. The massive sentry fell head first onto the floor, his own spear still clutched in cadaveric spasm in his muscular right hand!

Once again, Makohani ordered that the body be impaled on a wooden pole and displayed high-up over the overhanging cliffs for all the entire Kingdom to see.

All-in-all, there were eight attempts on his life over the years. Each one had been foiled by his cunning and ruthless internal security mechanisms. King Makohani was untouchable.

CHAPTER 12:

SOLITARY CONFINEMENT

The man with the rabbit foot around his neck was tasked with finding eagle hatchling for Makohani.

'There simply were no more eagle hatchlings to be found!' Explained Rabbit Foot.

He had arrived back empty-handed and Makohani was in a particularly foul mood.

'You mean to tell me you couldn't find me one single eagle hatchling!' said Makohani in disgust.

'They are all gone!' said Rabbit foot.

'Hmmmmmm.... I think you need to rest in my guest hut tonight! This will give you a chance to really decide if all the eagle hatchlings are all gone!' Said Makohani, as he motioned his sentries to carry away the exhausted Rabbit foot.

'Makohani's guest hut! They called it, *'was notorious and everyone feared it. Many a man and many a woman had found their ultimate fate in this very small mud-and-dung hut!'*

The walls were made of mud and dung. The floor was made of wood. The roof was made of thatch. There were no windows. No light could enter the hut and the only way to tell if it was day or night, was the heat! It was also raised high up above the ground on stilts.

Four sentries guarded the four corners of the 'guest hut' day and night. One meal a day and one calabash of water would be passed through the bottom of the front door. A small hole on the one side of the hut was used for waste purposes. There was no bed. The hut was simplicity itself.

Most men and women ended up dying in the hut. They usually died after about one week, usually from heat exhaustion. The reason they would die would be from increased heat or minimal fresh air to breathe. Sometimes the sentries themselves would forget to provide a meal or water to the prisoner.

Sometimes the prisoners would go mad, screaming wildly. When this happened, one of the sentries would simply enter the hut and thrust the prisoner with a spear, through-and-through the chest and heart. If it was a women, they would rape her, and then perhaps kill her. It all depended on the mood of the sentry on that particular day.

At times, Makohani would allow one of his many pet hyaenas into the hut and lock the door behind them. The hyaenas would then emerge, bloated, a few days later.

And now, Rabbit Foot was cast into this very hut, and the door was slammed shut behind him!

'I couldn't believe this punishment! All because I couldn't find him an eagle hatchling! The first thing that hits you in the hut is the smell! It is the smell of human sweat, faeces and fear!'

'Those two weeks were the toughest of my life!' he told Bo

'Day one was easy, day two was fine and day three is when your mind starts playing tricks on you! You start to imagine things. Time moves very (very!) slowly. One day feels like a week. There seems to be no hope. There is no hope! I tried to speak to my guards outside, but they ignored me completely! The only thing that was in my favour was that the guards liked me— so they continued to feed me and provide me with water.'

Bo watched the man's face as he recalled his time in the guest hut. He dared not interrupt his new friend.

'*My greatest fear was that Makohani would unleash his hyaenas in the hut with me!*' *This fear kept me sharp and vigilant! Thank goodness Makohani never decided to release his pet hyaenas into the hut – because then I surely would have been dead!*'

Bo watched the man frown as he continued. Bo could see from the expression on his face how hard it must have been in that hut.

'*And then I decided to plot my escape!*'

'*I finally dug my way through the thatch roof (at the top and in the one corner) and jumped the wall! I spent my time digging slowly through the thatch and hard clay earth with my fingernails. My fingertips bled! I worked as silently as I could without the guards hearing me. I worked mainly at night. I was nearly caught once or twice, yet I managed to conceal my escape*'.

'*Finally! Three days ago I escaped and I was busy fleeing when you came across me!*'

CHAPTER 13:

STRATEGY

The two men sat around the fire under the pitch-black sky.

Bo had killed a rock hyrax and the animal was being flame-roasted over the coals.

'We need to ponder and deliberate before we make our move', said Bo.

'Yes,' said Rabbit Foot, *'I am happy that I had the chance to carefully study Makohani and his sentries'.*

Bo took the roasted rock hyrax off the fire and placed it on a flat stone. He tore the one leg off, grabbed it between his index finger and middle finger and gave it to his new friend. *'What will enable us to strike and conquer, is foreknowledge.* Knowledge of Makohani and his men will give us an advantage. We know which of Makohani's sentries has the most ability and which of his men are most highly trained. His right-hand man, Maphuti, seems to be the brains behind Makohani's operations!'

'Yes, but Makohani is like a black mamba! Strike at its head, and you will be attacked by his tail; strike at his tail, and you will be attacked by his head; strike at his middle, and you will be attacked by both head and tail.'

'Then we must pretend to be weak, that the black mamba may grow arrogant! We must attack the black mamba when he is unprepared, we must appear where we are not expected'.

'Black mambas have angry tempers, we must therefore seek to irritate him'.

Bo tore the other roasted leg off for himself.

'We must keep ourselves continually on the move, and we must devise unfathomable plans.'

Rabbit foot looked swiftly at Bo. An idea has suddenly come to his mind.

'We need to walk to the next village and warn them of Makohani! We need to act swiftly in this matter. We need to get to them before Makohani's ants get to them!'

The two men sucked on the bones of their dinner, each lost in their own thoughts.

CHAPTER 14:

THE MANYUKI TRIBE

The Manyuki tribe lived on the shores of the great lake. They lived on the golden beach below the Mahale Mountain range. The women would walk into the surrounding forests by day collecting fruits and nuts and the men would go out and catch bush meat. Bush meat consisted chiefly of primates; although bushbuck and bush pig were also often caught. When they weren't in the forests, both men and women would be out on the vast lake catching fish.

Bo and Rabbit foot arrived wearily at about sunset at the tribal village. They literally stumbled right into the village. There was no formal greeting. No one even noticed the two young men. Life continued as per normal in the quiet little shore village.

'We need to see your Chief urgently!' Said Bo to the first adult they encountered.

The adult, a middle-aged African male with early male-pattern baldness and wearing only a pair of hessian-type shorts looked at the two men suspiciously.

'And why would you want to see our Chief?' he smiled an ironic smile, showing his few teeth in his mouth. The balding male was staring wide-eyed at the two newcomers and his nostrils flared a little as he called for some reinforcements from other villagers who were standing around.

'These two wish to see our Chief!' he said loudly for all to hear.

Bo and Rabbit foot stood quietly and humbly. They were both tired and both men were mentally and physically exhausted. They didn't really have time for this kind of attitude.

'Look! What is your name?' Asked Bo.

'I am Alfred,' said the man, proudly.

'Look Alfred. We need to see your Chief now or else many people will die!' Bo threatened the man.

'Why specifically do you want to see our Chief?' Alfred repeated his question.

Now there were a handful of spectators surrounding the three men.

'Your village is about to be invaded by King Makohani and his men! We have to warn your Chief!' screamed Bo, at the top of his voice.

The onlookers looked at one another shocked. And with this, a frail old man emerged from the crowd. He looked like one of the villagers. He was completely humble. He wore no special attire. There was no pomp or grandeur about him. He acted as if he were just another villager.

'Thank you Albert. I see these two young men. I am Godwaan, chief of the Manyuki tribe. My people call me *'inkunzi edla yodwa... Inkuzi emdwayidwa'*, the bull who eats alone and who has many scars from fighting...'

Bo could hardly believe that this little man was worthy of such a grand nickname, for he looked completely insignificant! He was of such small stature that he hardly had any presence at all! He would have been overlooked had he not been introduced!

'Please come, you two look tired. Let us have some food and drink and let us talk. You both are welcome.'

The villagers made a path and seemed to assist and help the two young men towards a central thatched region. The shaded canopy was fringed with coconut and papaya tees. The sand was covered with woven mats and the two were ushered to sit down and relax. Calabashes of fresh coconut juice were offered to the guests and banana leaves were offered to them with multiple small delicacies.

Godwaan proved to be a most-remarkable Chief! He was small, thin and slender built. He had grey scalp hair and his eyes had a ring-of-white around them, which portrayed a deep-seated wisdom. His body was lean and muscular. And, even though he was such a small man, he had a big spirit!

Bo and Rabbit Foot immediately liked him! They immediately felt they could trust him! They went on to discuss all they knew about King Makohani. The urgency in their voices made Godwaan realize that they were both speaking the truth. How had he not come to know of King Makohani?

'How do we not know about this King Makohani!?!' Godwaan scalded Alfred – the middle-aged African male who was the first person to meet Bo and Rabbit foot when they arrived in the village – It turns out that Alfred was supposed to be the *Head of Intelligence* for the village!

Alfred cast his eyes downwards in shame.

'Makohani's warrior's spirits were keenest in the morning; by noonday their spirits would begin to flag; and in the evening, their minds were only focussed on returning to the Kingdom. When his warriors stood leaning on their spears, they were faint from want of food.' Rabbit Foot was telling Godwaan.

'Therefore, if we were to attack them, it must be late noon!' Mused Godwaan.

Rabbit Foot went on to say that he had overheard Makohoni's warrior's discussing an invasion of the shore-lake tribes by the next moon!

'That is very soon!' Exclaimed Godwaan.

At this point, Bo interrupted.

'Chief Godwaan, Rabbit Foot, Alfred… Please. With all respect! I do not think that we must fight this man in the traditional manner! His warriors are skilled in warfare and all they know about is fighting. We will lose a lot of

lives if we were to go this way. We need to destroy King Makohani in a completely different way.'

Bo pleaded, 'Please! Let us sleep and let us think about this further. Tomorrow is another day. We can re-strategize then!'

And with this, all the men greeted and they all retired. That night, *restless waves* from the large lake lapped upon the shore.

CHAPTER 15:

THE PRINCE

It was actually Alfred, the Chief of Intelligence, who came up with the idea. He was feeling so downcast about having missed the existence of King Makohani that he went out of his way to try and salvage some form of his own self-dignity.

'I have an idea!' he stammered.

All three men were looking at Alfred who was still wearing the same pair of hessian-type shorts from the previous day.

'The best form of defence is attack! We therefore need to send Bo to meet with King Makohani. When Bo is close-up, he can personally kill King Makohani!'

'But how do we get Bo to meet with the King?' asked Rabbit Foot.

'We must transform Bo into someone important. Someone who cannot be ignored,' responded Godwaan.

'King Makohani will only meet with someone whom he considers a peer,' said Rabbit Foot.

Bo looked quietly at the men. His eyes flickered. He could see the wisdom behind this reasoning.

'Royalty!' he said.

'Prince Bo…' responded Godwaan *'…The Prince of Manyuki!'*

All three men looked at one another. The plan seemed a bit far-fetched, yet it was slowly beginning to unfold naturally before them.

'Your training will commence immediately!' said Godwaan. *'Alfred will be teaching you everything he knows about royalty and warfare. He may not look like much, but Alfred is actually our mightiest warrior!'*

Rabbit Foot looked at Bo suspiciously and raised his eyebrow.

CHAPTER 16:

THE TEACHINGS OF ALFRED SAMBURA

'As a lifelong practitioner of the art of war, I'm trained to remain calm in the face of adversity and danger,' Alfred begun his training session on the shore with these words.

It was hard to take him seriously though, what with his early male-pattern baldness and his only pair of hessian-type shorts. His body was scrawny and he had a face which looked somewhat naughty and mischievous.

Alfred was walking slowly past the two men, his hands clasped tightly behind his own back, when suddenly he lashed out and slapped Bo on the top of his head with an open hand.

"Ow!" Screamed Bo.

"How do you feel right now?" He asked with a smug air about him.

"It hurts!" Bo's eyes were watering with tears.

"You'll feel worse tomorrow!" Alfred smirked and continued walking.

"You need to try to understand what's out there," continued Alfred.

Alfred was clearly enjoying his role as teacher and it looked like Bo and Rabbit Foot were his first students ever.

"No matter how long you train someone to be brave – you never know if they are brave or not until something real happens." Alfred seemed to be speaking sense.

Alfred had changed direction and was walking back towards the two young men, his hands still clasped tightly behind his back.

'The most important thing is to think like the opposition and know where you're most at risk.' These words were aimed at Rabbit Foot, who knew King Makohani better than anyone.

At this point Rabbit Foot decided to break the rhythm! He stepped forward and interrupted the teaching session.

"King Makohani is not like any opponent you've ever dealt with before! I need to tell both of you a story of what exactly we are dealing with here." Rabbit Foot had such a serious look on his face that both Alfred and Bo gave him their undivided attention.

"The following was told to me by one of Makohani's men. The man's name has long been forgotten, although his story remains. Makohani was born with a blood clot grasped in his fist, a traditional sign that he was destined to become a great leader.

Apparently Makohani was abducted with 12 other young boys when he was thirteen-years-old and he was taken for ritual circumcision at an initiation school! Apparently they blindfolded the boys and took them somewhere far and remote on top of some mountain. The boy's parents didn't even know where they were! Apparently Makohani and the other boys all returned from that initiation ceremony one day later. The man told me that Makohani had cut the penises off ALL the elders! At thirteen years of age! Makohani had maimed and killed the elders of the initiation school! He had killed them with the same blade used to perform the ritual circumcision! Apparently he emerged from the mountain with 12 of the other boys.

For the next several months the boys wandered around the grasslands, surviving primarily on wild fruits and dead animal carcasses, rock hyrax, and other small game killed by the boys.

Their dedication towards Makohani from that day onwards was absolute, despite him being so young. They started off as a gang. Soon Makohani formalized their positions. They then became his advisors, sentries and warriors. His right hand man and friend was called Maphuti. He began his ascent by small-scale attacks on nomadic tribes. However these escalated over time. *What had begun as gang attacks on nomadic tribes soon became the wholesale massacre of civilian populations. What Makohani had started with his unofficial gang of loyal friends soon became a kingdom…"*

Alfred listened to this story in complete disbelief.

Bo too was stunned by what he heard.

"Your lessons are finished for today! You are both dismissed! It would appear that I need to re-strategize our training sessions!"

Rabbit Foot looked at Bo and Bo looked at Rabbit Foot. They were both speechless.

CHAPTER 17:

THE TEACHINGS OF CHIEF GODWAAN

The two young men were getting used to their new routine at the Manyuki tribal village.

Training with Alfred would take place every day, twice per day. He had re-strategized and adapted their training sessions. All aspects of their training had intensified.

Both men learned how to fight with their bare hands and with weapons.

Bo was very careful not to reveal his secret weapon, the poison-tipped arrow head, to anyone. Not even Rabbit Foot knew of his secret weapon! Bo had carefully broken off the distal tip of the arrow head and wrapped it twice in cloth and placed it very carefully at the bottom of his few personal possessions. It was so well hidden that he was certain no-one would ever find it.

Bo deeply understood that the tip of the arrow belonged in one place and one place only: within the heart of his enemy, King Makohani!

Alfred's teaching and training were exceptionally punishing on the body and both men were pushed well beyond their comfort zones.

At night, Chief Godwaan would teach Bo how a Prince should act, speak and behave. His teachings would focus chiefly on social graces and other upper class cultural rites as a preparation for entry into Royal society. Godwaan was clearly quite skilled in the art of etiquette. Bo was instructed on how to sit and walk and talk, for example.

The entire time, Godwaan's wives and daughters would be in the background watching the two young men, transfixed and mesmerized. One of Godwaan's daughter's, Nandy, would pay particular attention to Bo and smiled coyly and made eye contact with him from time to time. But Bo didn't really make much of this attention and concentrated on his learning.

"When I was young they used to call me *'inkomo edlayodwa' – the bull who eats alone.*" Begun Chief Godwaan. "It's not because I enjoyed solitude. It's because I tried to blend into the world before, and people disappointed me! I am a loner. In my head I wanted to feel that I can be anywhere. I craved silence and I craved solitude".

"So I left the world that I knew and started living by myself. But soon enough other people found me and they were attracted to my life and the way I was living peacefully on the banks of the shore. Before I knew it, I had a lot of people following me and living with me! Too many people! Soon we had to develop rules and laws. And so the Manyuki village was born!"

"Before I knew it, I became the Chief of the Manyuki Village!"

"A true leader knows how to treat others with respect and dignity!" Godwaan exclaimed.

"He practices empathy, generosity, and patience; while bringing lasting value to every relationship." Godwaan was advising Bo on the power of being a member of the Royalty. He revealed the secrets that every Royal should know in order to gain that extra polish and presence needed for his meeting with Makohani.

"But I am the son of poor villagers. I am but a herdsboy!" said Bo, despondent, *"How am I ever going to learn such skills in such a short time?"* His mood was low and he felt very despondent.

"A true leader should know exactly how to navigate any setting! A true leader must not demand respect – he must command respect!"

Bo looked around the room. The girls were giggling. His eyes were showing uncertainty.

"A true leader must also know how to eat and a true leader must also travel well! Food and travel must become an art!"

Dinner was served. The food looked and smelled delicious! Some of the tribal woman had walked into Godwaan's hut carrying a large wooden board covered with banana leaves. On the board was present a large sizzling bush pig! The pig was split down the middle and its juices oozed out, it was lying on banana leaves and it was roasted to perfection. Juices dripped onto the floor of the hut and the smell from the roast pork made everyone's mouth water and suddenly no-one could concentrate on the conversation anymore!

Bo and Rabbit Foot hadn't seen food like this in months and they just wanted to dive right in and tear off pieces of meat with their bare hands! They were both so tired and so hungry from their training that they had both, unknowingly, approached closer to the food.

"Stop!" Shouted Godwaan.

"When people have a willpower failure, it's because they haven't anticipated a situation what's going to come along. With self-discipline most anything is possible! You two have no willpower! You two have no self-discipline!"

Godwaan ordered that the pig be taken outside and that the villagers eat first from the pig.

"Bo and Rabbit Foot will eat what's left over of the pig at the end – after everyone has eaten! This will teach them willpower! By constant self-discipline and self-control you can develop greatness of character."

Bo looked at Rabbit Foot. Rabbit Foot looked at Bo. Once again, they were both speechless!

CHAPTER 18:

THE FIRST MOVE

Life continued at a relatively relaxed pace in the small shore line village. The woman worked hard, the children played hard and the men seemed to not do much at all – as was the normal rhythm in Africa.

However peace does not last forever. During the high moon, some seemingly nomadic thieves had entered their small village and had stolen some of the Manyuki tribe's maize and cattle!

Despite the best efforts to track the footprints of the thieves, the thieves were too clever and they seemed to have vanished into thin air!

Bo and Rabbit Foot realized that Makohani's attack had begun! *So soon!* They were hardly finished with their training yet! Their training was still in its earliest days!

'What are we going to do about the theft?' asked one of the villagers to Chief Godwaan.

'Our supplies are already in short supply' exclaimed another.

There was much talk under the central thatch hut that day and the African sun burned fiercely through the sky.

Alfred suggested they build better barriers which would hopefully deter the thieves.

The villagers decided that this was an excellent idea and they helped collect thorn branches. The villagers used the branches to reinforce their precious cattle and to protect their precious supply of maize.

"The thieves will attack again in a few days!" Rabbit Foot warned the villagers.

"We need to act now!" cried one of Godwaan's daughters. *"We need to introduce King Makohani to the Prince of Manyuki as soon as possible!'*

Obviously, the situation was very tense and the entire village was under threat.

The situation was so worrisome that Chief Godwaan called an immediate meeting with Alfred and the two men.

"We know what is happening in our village, for it happened to both of your villages. We must therefore thank you for warning and saving our people! It is time for us to act. We must see that history does not repeat itself!"

Godwaan, called a tribal meeting. It was now the time that he introduced the Prince to his people.

CHAPTER 19:

THE COUNTER MOVE

Several days later the Prince of Manyuki would arrive at Makohani's Kingdom, ostensibly dressed in the finest of garments. He would be followed by an entourage of his faithful servants.

"When the Prince speaks, it must be like flowers blooming, seas rolling back, doors opening and one must be able to smell the smell of a valley of fresh flowers!" Alfred reminded Bo.

His right hand man, Rabbit Foot, would wear a painted face, so as that no-one would recognize him for whom he really was.

The Prince would arrive in a magnificent cattle-drawn carriage, pulled by eight cattle. He would be adorned in spectacular necklaces, bracelets and the finest of silks. All his servants would seem to admire and respect him and they would walk obediently behind his carriage.

Rumors of this strange Prince's wondrous and good fortune would reach Makohani's Kingdom several days before his arrival. There would be great anticipation and excitement about the Prince's arrival.

Upon arrival, he would display ever-increasingly impressive spectacles for the warriors at the foot-hills of Makohani's mountain Kingdom.

One such spectacle would entail the Prince arriving to the sound of a mesmerizing drum beat. Bo's entourage had multiple drums and all his men would beat a haunting, dramatic and rhythmic beat, which mimicked the sound of the human heart beat – as they made their way slowly upwards towards the kingdom. The beating drums were accompanied by a deep and low guttural humming from the men who travelled with him in the entourage.

Another such spectacle would entail an 'arrival gift' for each and every warrior. These gifts consisted of precious stones. There were so many precious stones on the shores of the lakeside village that it simply was no problem to load these gemstones onto the carriage and present them to each and every soldier upon arrival at the Kingdom!

"Behold his excellency, Prince Manyuki!" Rabbit Foot announced*!" "We come in peace. We come to meet your King. We come to establish trade. We come in good spirits. We come with open heart!"*

The warriors met the entourage with what could only be described as a mixture of great excitement and animation. They were briefed of his arrival and King Makohani did appear to be expecting them!

They were ushered upwards towards the mountain to meet the King himself.

A multitude of warriors led them up to the *Vulture's Nest.*

CHAPTER 20:

THE VULTURES NEST

The top secret, high security site was located in the mountains about half a day's walk from the foothills. Three security zones surrounded the central hut, which were guarded by Makohani's fiercest soldiers.

Over 3000 men worked day and night, winter and summer, for 13 moons to complete the project. The path was hacked into the mountainside, passing through five tunnels to get to the entrance.

Heavy wooden gates guarded the opening and Makohani's main hut was located on the summit, which gave a grand view of all the surrounding regions.

Such a marvel of architecture was unheard of in that time. Makohani surely must have been a great visionary in order to build such a magnificent site.

Both Bo and Rabbit Foot were stunned with what they saw! Each foot step going upwards towards the nest appeared perfectly manicured. The detail of the foot stones is what blew them away. Each foot stone had unique and ornate markings and there were thousands of them! Each stone was designed, crafted and laid by hand. Such craftsmanship was unknown in that time.

After several hours travelling up the mountain, the entire entourage had to rest. They were already quite far up the mountain. The height was dizzying!

'I can see why they call this place the vultures nest!' said one of the servants pointing to several of the big grey birds which were nesting on the nearby cliffs and which were soaring in the air, swishing past the delegation, regarding them with their lifeless, dark and bead-like eyes.

Bo used this opportunity to feel for his arrow head, which was still concealed and wrapped tightly in cloth and which was held very close to his person, amongst his personal belongings.

The delegation continued winding their way up the mountain path. The air seemed to be getting thinner towards the top. Or perhaps it was the anticipation of meeting the man himself – King Makohani!

CHAPTER 21:

THE DELEGATION ARRIVES

When the delegation finally arrived, the first thing that struck them was the view. It was magnificent! One could see clearly from horizon to horizon. It felt as if they were located on the highest point in Africa.

A group of young maidens arrived, they bowed and they were submissive and they led the delegation to their huts to settle down. No-where was King Makohani to be seen! Both Bo and Rabbit Foot knew that they were being watched and observed though.

The entire delegation was housed in four separate guest huts which were built on the edge of the mountainous cliff. Vultures continued to soar past their huts, getting ready to nest, as the day started to become dusk.

A blanket of cloud and mist had also started to move in, quietly, obscuring the foothills below the mountainous village, as early night began to set in. Still no obvious signs of King Makohani could be seen.

Prince Bo and Rabbit Foot and his servants had settled into their huts and now emerged, tired and hungry. The soldiers who had accompanied them up the mountain were gone. The maidens who had shown them their accommodation were also nowhere to be found.

An eerie wind blew through the mountainous village as all members of the delegation looked at one another.

Bo felt uneasy.

"Behold his excellency, Prince Manyuki!" Rabbit Foot announced on the top of his voice!" *"We come in peace. We come to meet your King. We come to establish trade. We come in good spirits. We come with open heart!"*

Rabbit Foot repeated the welcome again, his voice trying to sound hopeful and welcoming.

No response.

They were alone. Alone on top of the mountain. Bo ordered that his men search the area for someone. Anyone.

Yet, there was not a soul present. There was nothing to eat. There was nothing to drink.

Time seemed to continue very slowly. There was tense anguish in the air.

'Tonight we sleep in these huts on the top of this mountain!' Bo ordered everyone. *'We need to get some rest. Tomorrow is another day and we will decide what to do first thing tomorrow morning!* He also ordered that the cattle be tied up.

With that, all men cast uneasy looks at one another. The silence on the top of the mountain was deafening. Rabbit Foot didn't like the look of this and suspected that something evil was afoot.

'Our Prince is right!' echoed Rabbit Foot. He attempted to conceal his doubt and his fears.

'Tonight we get some rest and tomorrow we decide what to do.'

Bo, Rabbit Foot and Alfred went to sleep in the one hut, and all the other men went to sleep in the other huts.

CHAPTER 22:

DAY BREAK ON THE TOP OF THE MOUNTAIN

By morning, Bo, Rabbit Foot and Alfred awoke after a restless night. They exited the hut before the sun shot through the darkness. Alfred went to wake the other members of the delegation, only to find that none of them were there! They were all gone!

Rabbit Foot and Bo were also soon coming to the realization that Makohani's soldiers had dispatched of his team during the course of the night. They must have done it swiftly and silently, because none of the three men heard even the slightest sound during the night!

Rabbit Foot was looking at the spoor on the ground. There must have been over 20 soldiers present that night. They had stealthily walked amongst the huts and abducted and killed their fellow men!

Alfred was the most affected by this realization! He began to break down and tears filled his eyes! He was so overwhelmed with emotion that he could not speak.

Bo needed to dig deep and provide some sort of leadership in the moment.

'We need to stand our ground!' said Bo, quietly and with absolute self-belief.

Suddenly, the man himself strode quietly and confidently down one of the foot paths. Like a big male lion he strutted. He was flanked by at least twelve of his men.

Prince Bo, Rabbit Foot and Alfred stood their ground; all were in fear and awe of this man, this Makohani...

"Breast milk, semen, sweat, tears and mucous are not created when we are calm and reasonable" began Makohani.

"I can sense that your juices are drying up!" He scoffed

Alfred, Bo and Rabbit Foot were stunned into silence and submission by this introduction. They both stared silently at the King who was wearing a lion skin around his shoulders and a leopard skin around his pelvis and he was flanked by his warriors.

"Welcome to my Vulture's Nest!" continued Makohani.

"Vultures are untameable, yet I have succeeded in training mine to follow me everywhere and let me catch them whenever I want to." Makohani began, *"I can't come atop my mountain without one or two or three of them immediately perching on my arms or on my head. I have always taken pleasure in taming wild animals. I want them to love me - yet still feel free!"*

"Where are my men?" Shouted Bo.

"Your men are down below. We helped them down the mountain in the middle of the night. Some of them even tried to fly like my vultures, although only for a short time!"

Rabbit Foot and Alfred felt sick listening to this madman speak. He had a full-blown God-complex and a heart of pure evil.

"Why? My men did nothing to you!" shouted Bo.

"Do you think that I'm an infant!?" asked Makohani in a mocking tone.

"Do you think that I am stupid?" he asked in a higher tone of voice.

"Do you think that you could fool me?" King Makohani mocked.

"Today is going to be the worst day of your lives! Today I am going to torture and kill each and every one of you. And my entire kingdom will get the pleasure of watching you three vermin die!"

With these words Makohani's warriors descended upon the three men and tied their wrists tightly behind their backs with thick brown leather.

Makohani watched his orders being executed dispassionately, while a lone vulture swooped low over the group, eyeing them with its beady eye.

CHAPTER 23:

TORTURE AND PUNISHMENT

All three men were marched down the steep mountain path. Bodies of their fellow men lay strewn and splattered amongst the rocks on the steep downhill pathway. Some of the vultures had descended *en masse* and were feeding on the bodies of the fallen men. Bo had tears in his eyes. Rabbit Foot seemed to immediately understand his fate. Alfred, too was struck dumb and silent.

When they finally arrived at base camp, the message was communicated to the entire Kingdom that King Makohani had captured some would-be assassins. By mid-day, all would be invited to watch their public execution. The general mood in the Kingdom seemed to buzz like a beehive. The Kingdom's desire to witness punishment was far too thrilling to miss!

All three men were tied with their wrists tight behind their backs to wooden poles which were driven deeply into the earth by Makohani's strongest warriors. The leather was bound so tightly around Bo's wrists that it cut deeply into his skin, his hands began to feel numb and he could feel the warm blood trickling down his hands.

The crowds continued to gather. All three men looked at one another with dead and defeated eyes. They had all been stripped of their possessions. Bo didn't even know what they had done with his few personal possessions, let alone the carefully broken off distal tip of the arrow head which was wrapped twice in cloth and placed very carefully at the bottom of his few personal possessions.

Soon it was mid-day. The sun was high in the sky. It was hot and the temperature was oppressing. The crowd had gathered in their droves. There was much animation and commotion in the air. The scene was set for high entertainment and the crowds were hungry!

Bo scanned the crowd for anyone from his old village, yet he could not recognize anyone amidst the masses. What did Makohani do to all the women and children he kidnapped from his tribe? He asked himself.

The first victim would be Rabbit Foot. Makohani had recognized him! His torture would be the first. Rabbit Foot was to be *'quartered'*.

The plan was to first have Rabbit Foot emasculated. Makohani himself cut off Rabbit Foots external genitalia. The remains, of which, were held high up by Makohani who grinned widely, he shook Rabbit Foot's bloody genitals about and displayed them prominently across the village. The villagers went wild at this sight!

After this horrible preliminary, a rope was attached to each of Rabbit Foot's limbs, one being bound round each leg from the foot to the knee, and round each arm from the wrist to the elbow. These ropes were then fastened to four bars, to each of which a strong male bull was harnessed, as if for towing a plough. These cattle were first made to give short jerks; and when the agony had elicited heart-rending cries from the unfortunate Rabbit Foot, who felt his limbs being dislocated without being broken, the four cattle were all suddenly whipped and urged on in different directions, and thus all Rabbit Foot's limbs were strained at one moment.

However Rabbit Foot's tendons and ligaments still resisted strongly the combined efforts of the four cattle, he resisted valiantly! So Makohani's sentries assisted, and they made several 'cuts' with a hatchet on each joint. When at last, each of the four cattle had traumatically amputated a limb, they were collected and placed near

Rabbit Foot's hideous trunk, which still showed signs of life!

Rabbit Foot was wheezing and coughing blood. He was in so much pain. His eyes were white with fear and pain. Blood oozed from his shoulder joints and his hip joints. Blood also trickled from the place where his genitals used to be. The crowd was cheering wildly and they were clearly thirsty for more!

Makohani stepped over the trunk of Rabbit Foot. He then disembowelled the poor man with his knife. Bo and Alfred couldn't watch as they realized that Rabbit Foot was still alive! Because as Makohani inserted the blade into Rabbit Foots abdomen, Rabbit Foot screamed and flexed his trunk!

Makohani continued to disembowel Rabbit Foot and he told his henchmen to suspend the trunk, and tie it, with its own intestines, to a wooden pole.

The cries from the crowd were deafening. How could they be enjoying this? Rabbit Foot had done nothing to deserve such cruelty. Rabbit Foot had done nothing to these crowds of people. Bo could hardly hear himself think. Alfred had already resigned himself to his fate. Alfred's head just hung low as he stared at the ground.

Makohani's hands were covered in blood. He wiped them on a cloth and stood up tall and proud to address the crowds.

"We are going to take a break for lunch now! We will be back after lunch for the other two!"

The crowd cheered wildly, they were very much amused, and there was much animation.

Bo looked at the remains of Rabbit Foot, already the vultures were descending upon the body parts, and there were flies buzzing on the oozing blood.

"Poor Rabbit Foot. Poor poor Rabbit Foot." Whimpered Bo to Alfred.

And with this, Bo noticed a little old man amidst the crowd. He looked like one of the villagers. He was completely humble. He wore no special attire. There was no pomp or grandeur about him. He acted as if he were just another villager. It was Godwaan, chief of the Manyuki tribe! The small man whose nickname was *'inkunzi edla yodwa... Inkuzi emdwayidwa'*, the bull who eats alone and who has many scars from fighting... He was in the crowd! He had secretly infiltrated Makohani's Kingdom and he winked *slyly* at Bo!

Suddenly, there was but the smallest chance of hope.

CHAPTER 24:

THE BULL WHO EATS ALONE

Godwaan received his nickname *'inkunzi edla yodwa…
Inkuzi emdwayidwa'* (*the bull who eats alone and who has
many scars from fighting*), when he was a younger man.

Godwaan was like an old bull buffalo that had been
kicked out of the herd and spent all day wallowing in mud.
He had a really short temper and it was best to stay away
from him. These days he had become much more serene
and tranquil though and hardly ever lost his temper. Only
the scars from previous fights marred his body, face and
soul.

After years of conflict, Godwaan's face was like that of
an old buffalo. It was scarred with emotions. Even though
he was a small man with diminutive stature, his presence
shone through. His eyes betrayed a deep wisdom.

Bo gestured to Godwaan to come closer. Bo was still
tightly tied to the wooden pole. His wrists were tied tightly
behind his back. The rope was cutting deep into his wrists.
His hands were bloody.

"Godwaan!" Bo whispered.

*"Please get my personal possessions. I need them!
Please try and find them for me! There is a poison arrow
tip inside. Please get me that arrow tip!"*

Godwaan seemed to understand immediately. He had
watched Bo secretly guard his possession when he first
arrived at the Manyuki tribe. He could sense that there was

something important within his possessions. Also, the way Bo always seemed to have his possessions around constantly seemed to hint to Godwaan of something of great importance therein.

Godwaan could see Bo's possessions hidden behind one of the African huts. There were two large Africans standing near his possessions and it seemed as if they were not going to move away. Godwaan had to get hold of Bo's belongings!

Godwaan decided to use distraction. The classic physical method as used by pickpockets. He understood that there were many classic military strategies based upon distraction. For example, throw a force at a weak point, making the other side rush troops to the rescue, then you apply your main force to the point they have just abandoned.

The principles of distraction were all the same. Distract by using the basic rules of sensation, whilst simultaneously and gently slipping past their guard. Godwaan would use the ultimate distraction: Women!

Gondwaan approached two relatively attractive young maidens in the crowd and told them that Makohani had asked them to carry water to his mountain spa. Godwaan then approached the two African males and told them that Makohani would appreciate if they would escort the two young maidens to his mountain spa. The story was eminently plausible, because Rabbit Foot had told them that this was a normal part of the ritual within Makohani's Kingdom.

The matter was so easily executed and the men were so easily distracted that Godwaan easily managed to collect Bo's belongings and he had all the time in the world to inspect the contents.

CHAPTER 25:

THE TIP OF A SPEAR

Godwaan found the broken-off distal tip of the arrow wrapped in cloth. He knew that this is what Bo wanted. And he managed to secretly pass the wrapped arrow tip to Bo's hands – even though they were still tied behind his back!

Bo was holding the small piece of cloth, the arrow tip neatly wrapped within, despite the fact that his wrists were tied tightly to the pole behind his back.

Makohani and his henchmen had returned from lunch. There was much animation as he took the central stage. The villagers had all gathered around once again. Makohani looked at Alfred and he looked at Bo. He then raised both his arms into the air.

"Who shall be next?" he asked.

"Who shall we teach next?" he implored, even louder.

The crowds were becoming more and more animated. It shocked Bo that the crowd were calling for their blood. How could crowds be whipped up into a frenzy such as this? How could the crowds not realize that this was wrong? How come no-one in the crowds could stop this madness? Bo had done no evil to any of the villagers – yet they were calling for his blood! And poor Alfred, poor, sweet old Alfred, the most harmless man on earth! And poor, poor Rabbit Foot! They most certainly did not deserve this treatment!

"Let us let the Ancestors decide!" screamed Makohani. The crowd cheered.

With that he plucked a feather off his neck collar. He held the feather up high in the air. He slowly released the grip on the feather. And the wind blew the feather directly to Alfred.

"The Ancestors have decided!"

"This old man will be the next to learn the lessons of Makohani!"

"No!" screamed Bo!

"Leave the old man alone! I will go next! The old man has done nothing!" I will go next!"

Makohani was surprised at this sudden bravery from the young man.

"Whip him!" Said Makohani to his chief henchman.

The henchman unleashed a cracking whip onto Bo's naked back. The sound split the air just as it split the skin on his back. Bo suffered the pain in silence. His body stiffened.

"Whip him again!" ordered Makohani.

The sentries lifted the whip up high again. And he bought it down fast and hard upon Bo's buttocks and hands. It nearly whipped the arrow-within-the-cloth from his grip! Once again the crack split the air and Bo screeched with pain.

"We will teach the Old Man next – as the Ancestors have suggested!" Alfred's head still hung low in defeat. Who knew what was going through his mind? His eyes were dead. He had given up hope. The crowd cheered wildly!

Makohani had devised a particularly cruel method for Alfred.

Makohani would use *Giant African Cane Rats!*

Makohani realized that this was a cheap and effective way to torture someone.

The sentries dragged Alfred from his pole. He didn't even put up a fight! The sentries placed Alfred inside a wooden barrel, with only his head exposed. He was completely restrained within the barrel, which was tied to the ground. Next, they made many superficial slits and cuts in his stomach. Alfred winced every time the knife incised him! He was now oozing blood from the superficial wounds.

The crowd was mesmerized. Makohani walked around, hands behind his back, arrogant, observing and delegating to his sentries. There was much focus on poor Alfred's face when they eventually had him strapped inside the barrel.

"Now bring the Giant African Cane Rats!" cried Makohani.

One of the sentries suddenly came running excitedly from behind with a wooden crate filled with approximately four giant brown African cane rats. Each rat was the size of a small dog. Ugly – with golden brown fur and the sharpest of teeth.

The crowd gasped at this spectacle.

Makohani raised the wooden box up high above his head for the whole crowd to see. The four starving rats peaked their whiskered heads from their wooden crate. Very soon they would be gnawing their victim from inside the barrel.

Bo felt sick and vomited on the ground in front of him! The crowd continued with their collective frenzy. Makohani knew exactly how to capture the crowd's imagination.

Makohani began singing a song, which whipped the crowd up even more as he walked around parading the heavy rats high up in the air! The song was a haunting and enigmatic old war song, designed to capture the hearts and minds of his people.

The song reverberated within the souls of his people, to the beating drums in the background.

"What have we done? He sung. *"Is this the truth?"* He sung. *"Why are we killed?"* He sung. *"Return Africa"* He sung.

Makohani was so caught up in the moment. He was so hypnotized with his own singing that he hardly realised how close he was to Bo! Makohani was within inches of where Bo was tied to the pole!

Bo dropped the cloth and held the poison-tipped-arrow-head tight within his hands. The point was pointed outwards. He swung around swiftly in an arch around the pole and scratched Makohani on his thigh! Bo could feel the arrow tip scratch the King on his thigh.

Makohani was so lost in the moment what with his singing and his chanting, the Giant Brown African Cane Rats still held high above his head – that he didn't even notice the little scratch upon his leg!

Alfred still stared at the ground. Expressionless, he waited for the brown rats to begin gnawing into his intestines. He could imagine the first few hours of agonizing pain which would surely result in his death. Alfred began crying.

Just as Makohani approached Alfred and the barrel, a pale look appeared in his eyes. Suddenly and swiftly Makohani dropped like a sack of potatoes. Dead! The crate containing the Giant African Cane Rats shattered on the earth and the brown vermin scattered everywhere, like dogs, they escaped.

"It worked!" Thought Bo, before collapsing to the base of his pole.

CHAPTER 26:

TWO YEARS LATER

Each storm has a beginning-, a middle- and an end.

It was as if a huge pressure had suddenly been released. The change from dictatorship to democracy was beyond joyous. There was much celebration in those first few weeks and it was as if Utopia had suddenly appeared. Suddenly, the violent dictator Makohani was gone and the villagers were free.

Makohani was the Authority and the villagers believed in him and obeyed him. Makohani had the assistance of his henchmen, he had the material resources and, most importantly, there were those sadistic punishments of those who were disobedient.

The question naturally arose, who would take over once his dictatorship fell? What would prevent the rise of a new dictator? Godwaan, Alfred and Bo wanted to ensure that Makohani was not replaced by a newer and more evil dictator.

The people's emotions were still very raw. They didn't understand the term democracy. They had no idea of this thing and they would need to be guided.

Godwaan had already secretly determined which aspects of Makohani's rule had to be abolished and which needed to be revised. He had in mind what measures had to be put in place to improve life for the villagers. He also had a clear vision of the long-term efforts needed to create a new society.

Now that the fear had been removed, the villagers were free. The formerly oppressed villagers had now developed more self-confidence. However, the sad reality was that not all men can handle such freedom.

Due to the fact that Makohani had decimated so many small villages, the tribal units in the surrounding lands had been fractured. There were people from many different tribes living together in one Kingdom. These people had no villages left to return to, for all those villagers had been slaughtered by Makohani and his henchmen. These people simply had nowhere left to go. They simply now formed part of this new kingdom.

Within a space of two years, Godwaan had become the new temporary ruler of Makohani's Kingdom. Just as clouds settled into their natural position, so too, Godwaan had naturally settled into his new position. The people seemed to enjoy and respect him. It was his humility which impressed them most. And Godwaan proved to be a most-remarkable leader, despite his small, thin and slender build. For such a small man, he had a big spirit!

"Your health and your happiness are dependent on your habits!" Godwaan was famed for saying. He wanted to get all his people into good new habits. Godwaan realized that a few well-chosen words at just the right time could transform a person's life.

The entire Manyuki tribe, who lived on the shores of a great lake, on the golden beach below the Mahale Mountain range joined Godwaan's new Kingdom. Godwaan's new Kingdom now counted 10 000 strong!

Alfred had become his chief advisor. It was still hard to take him seriously though, what with his early male-pattern baldness and those hessian-type shorts – which he still wore! His body was still scrawny and his face had aged somewhat. The wounds which Makohani had inflicted upon his body had now healed into thick keloid scars.

Bo had become Gondwaan's second in command. He had married Godwaan's eldest daughter, Nandi. The entire relationship had developed very quickly within the first few months after Makohani's death. Bo couldn't believe that he now had a wife and that she was now pregnant with his child! This made Bo very happy and he smiled secretly to himself. Bo had suffered unimaginable hardship and losses in his short life. And now, suddenly, he was a free man, a husband and soon-to-be a father!

The arrow-tip-laced-with-butterfly-poison, which had unleashed their freedom, had been framed and mounted and stood on display in Makohani's old residence, which was located on the top of the Vultures Nest. Godwaan had ordered that the residence become a memorial/museum for all those who lost their lives at the hand of the tyrant called Makohani.

The arrow tip had become symbolic of the Manyuki tribes freedom and new value system. It was a sacred item which was to be revered by the entire kingdom. It was this arrow tip which had defeated the tyranny of King Makohani. As such, two guards were placed at the entrance to the door of the museum in which it was now guarded. It was to be guarded day and night. The arrow tip was to become a shrine to democracy and the end of dictatorship. Once a year the arrow tip would be removed and paraded around the entire Kingdom as a reminder of their communal history.

Soon, the natural rhythm of Africa returned. The sun poured down from the sky and over the vast tribal lands. The women collected fruits and nuts by day and the men tended their cattle and would go out and catch bush meat from time to time. Both men and women would go to the vast lake to catch fish every now and again.

Unfortunately, good weather doesn't last forever. Another storm was busy forming on the horizon.

CHAPTER 27:

WITHOUT A TRACE

What had become of Makohani's sentries? What had become of the henchmen who formed part of his elite inner circle? What had become of the men who had carried out Makohani's evil orders and policies? What had become of those who were now being accused of war crimes and crimes against humanity?

Godwaan, Alfred and Bo had mused on these matters. There were very clear signals from the community that these perpetrators of evil were not wanted amongst them. Godwaan, Alfred and Bo had tried to remain vigilant after assuming power. They spoke to- and with the villagers. Many of the villagers were kidnapped by these self-same perpetrators from their own villages, which were burned to the ground.

Godwaan understood the dangers of having a small glowing ember. For a single glowing ember could re-ignite and burn down an entire kingdom!

So Godwaan ordered the following: He ordered that all twelve of Makohani's highest-ranking sentries, including Maphuti – his right-hand man, were to be immediately put to death. Incidentally, one of Makohani's highest-ranking henchman immediately committed suicide upon hearing this order! He had hung himself within his hut from one of the lowest-wooden beams. The rest – including Maphuti – were to be executed in front of the whole Kingdom the following day. They would simply be hung from their necks and allowed to die. Black bags were placed over their heads in shame and they were hung one by one. The bodies were present for all to see and the vultures feasted on them for weeks. The villagers were only too glad to help with the sentries' removal.

The rest of Makohani's lower ranking sentries were pardoned, provided that they helped re-shape their new society for the better.

Many of the other sentries had simply argued that they had simply been following orders. Godwaan however ruled that 'following orders' was not a legitimate defence for their criminal acts.

Some of the perpetrators and collaborators were never brought to justice though. Many of them returned to the jobs that they had left before Makohani's came into power. Many of them continued with their lives as if nothing had ever happened. They ended up working side-by-side with the same people they had once oppressed!

Godwaan had taken the route of 'benevolent dictator'. He still ruled with an iron fist – although in a nicer and softer way. He proved to be authoritarian leader exerting absolute political power over the villagers but for the benefit of the population as a whole. Godwaan allowed for some democratic decision-making to exist – but with limited power. Godwaan was viewed by the villagers as an 'enlightened despot'.

Under Godwaan's new leadership, the kingdom was known to be relatively free from corruption, stable, and safe, particularly when compared to its former self. Under Godwaan's rule, the kingdom had seemed to have modernized and had experienced a vast increase in the quality of life.

Yet it was surprising how everyone was still affected by Makohani's legacy long after his death! It had been two years since Makohani's death and the people still lived in fear as if he were still in power! The people were still very submissive and acted as if they were opressed. The people still walked around in fear and still talked in fear. It was as if the invisible hand of Makohani still ruled over them!

It was almost as if Godwaan had inherited a dog which had been whipped and beaten into complete submission. This dog was weak and psychologically beaten. It walked with its tail tucked tightly between its legs. This dog would even urinate and defecate in fear!

Such a population proved very easy to rule. They were tamed. Godwaan had no problems coming up with new laws and regulations. And everyone seemed to obey the new laws. There was no obstruction or defiance from any of the people. Everyone just seemed to 'get along' and it seemed almost as if there was peace in the land.

It seemed as if the society had begun to re-build itself and it seemed as if the wounds were starting to heal. Even the fractured bones of the society were starting to knit and people were starting to fill up their lives once again.

Which is why the sudden disappearance of the poisoned-arrow-tip from its resting place up high on the Vulture's Nest, caused such a sudden and severe panic amongst the masses! Despite it being under constant guard!

Godwaan, Alfred and Bo decided to call an urgent public meeting. All the villagers from the kingdom and/or representatives were to attend.

"Our sacred arrow-tip has disappeared!" exclaimed Godwaan to all the people.

"Our arrow tip which symbolizes our freedom is gone! Our arrow-tip which killed your former ruler has suddenly disappeared without a trace! It was resting inside the museum on the top of Vulture's Nest, guarded by two guards, and yesterday, it was noticed to have disappeared! If anyone has any information about the whereabouts of our arrow-tip, please let us know!"

There was much animation about the crowds. One could sense the shock and surprise this news had suddenly caused.

Godwaan continued further: *"We are willing to offer a reward to anyone who comes to us with information regarding our missing arrow head! This arrow head is sacred to our Kingdom!"*

And with that, Bo, Alfred and Godwaan thanked the people for their time and slowly, and wearily, departed.

As they walked away, Alfred spoke to Godwaan and Bo under his breath:

"I fear that one of Makohani' ex-sentries are behind this theft. Bo, until this very day you have never shared with us the secret origin of the poison of your arrow tip. I fear that you may have to get us some more of that poison! I fear that one of Makohani's sentries is still alive and is planning a coup and we need to be prepared! Even though we lined them all up and killed them all, there may be one or two who are still alive!

Godwaan had a deep frown upon his forehead and Bo was just walking head hanging low. Bo now had a wife and an unborn child to consider. He looked at Godwaan and he looked at Alfred.

"I will fetch us some more poison! I will leave the kingdom at once! First let me wish my Nandy farewell" Bo had an intense, yet sad, look in his eyes.

CHAPTER 28:

THE BUTTERFLY LARVAE

Bo loved Nandy very deeply and he could hardly express his love for her in words. He approached her with much trepidation. Saying farewell to his woman was not going to be easy. His heart hung heavy in his chest. Bo entered the hut silently and Nandy was busy cleaning. She looked so beautiful with her small pregnant belly. Her soft skin was so soft, so silky and so feminine.

"Greetings my lady" said Bo.

"Greetings my man" responded Nandy.

Bo went up close to his lady and grabbed her around her waist. She was so light and so beautiful. Her hair was so dark and her soul was so deep. When she smiled at Bo, it was as if the whole world stood still. And Bo loved the way she smelled. *He could breathe her in forever!*

"My lady", began Bo, *"My lady, I have some heavy news…"*

"What is it my man?" she asked with wide, deep and innocent eyes.

"I have to go on an important mission." He said hesitantly.

"I have to go and find the secret poison that I used for the arrow tip. I have to go and find the secret poison used to kill Makohani. Alfred fears that one of Makohani's sentries is alive and is going to attack us! Godwaan fears that there will be a coup! It is for this reason that I have to

go back and get some more of the secret poison that also killed my cousin the day he was washing in the river."

"*I understand my love!*" she said, while turning and holding her belly with two hands. Bo could not see the single tear trickling from her left eye.

"*Please just go safe and please come back safe!*" she sounded more firm. It was as if she suddenly understood what was at stake here.

Bo would have to find those deep impenetrable forests of Central Eastern Africa. Bo would have to locate the mountain range covered in thick clouds and mists. He would have to find the stream in the forest where the waters bubbled clear.

But first, he would spend the night tightly embraced within the arms of his loving wife and his unborn child.

CHAPTER 29:

MAPHUTI

Maphuti – the late Makohani's highest-ranking sentry and right-hand man didn't travel far.

His escape was ingenious! When Godwaan's men slipped the black bags over their heads, he had managed, by means of his allies, to switch himself out for another with a black bag over his head! This all happened behind the scenes, without anyone's knowledge. The poor fool who died in his place was an old cobbler from his village. Maphuti still had powerful connections and allies within the Kingdom.

He had set up camp not too far away from the Vulture's nest. He knew full well that he was labelled as a war criminal. He understood the atrocities which he had helped commit. He still had a yearning for his previous way of life. He had become addicted to power and his lifestyle and he didn't really feel at all responsible for his wrongdoings – after all, he was merely following orders!

He had found a nearby cave, which was located about a day's walk from the Vulture's nest. He had made certain that there were no obvious signs of his presence. He only made a fire within the cave at night so as that no one would ever see the smoke from the fire. He even made extra special care of not leaving any footprints when he walked. He was skilled in highly dangerous military anti-tracking tactics. He was, after all, personally responsible for Makohani's elite guard.

Maphuti had realized the power of the arrow tip and he had stolen it one moonless night. It was so easy to steal! The two guards were protecting it from the front of the museum. Maphuti had secretly entered from the back of the museum! *'What fools!'* he thought. Maphuti had realized that this self-same weapon which had ended Makohani's rule would be the self-same weapon which would commence his rule! Maphuti caressed the arrow head in his thick-calloused hands and scoffed at himself.

The plan was to use the self-same arrow-tip on Godwaan, Alfred and Bo and re-claim Makohani's Kingdom for himself! Why the Kingdom needed a foreign ruler was strange to Maphuti! Maphuti understood how Makohani's Kingdom worked. Maphuti understood what the people expected from a ruler. These insights, he mused, would take an outsider such as Godwaan years to understand! Maphuthi argued that he should have been promoted to leader. Maphuti argued that he could have eased into his new responsibilities effortlessly. Maphuti understood that Godwaan had no bearings on his new role. Maphuti knew that Godwaan simply had to be removed.

That night, around the cave fire, deep in the dark, dank cavern, he conspired with himself. The flames flickered on the walls and he spoke to himself in a hushed voice. He had killed a warthog earlier that day and it was roasting on the fire.

"Tomorrow I will go quietly back to the Kingdom. I will be wearing peasants clothing and I will hide my face. It is likely that Godwaan, Alfred and Bo will be living up on the Vultures Nest. It is therefore important that I get there soon and stab and kill all three with this arrow head!"

Maphuti held the arrow head tight in his right fist. He then begun drumming a beat with his hands on his chest, he had begun singing Makohani's old war song to himself. The song was haunting and enigmatic and it filled the walls of the cave with an aura of war. The song reverberated within his soul, to the beating of his chest in the background.

"*What have we done?* He sung. *"Is this the truth?"* He sung. *"Why are we killed?"* He sung. *"Return Africa"* He sung.

The warthog was ready for eating.

CHAPTER 30:

THE STRANGE COINCIDENCE

The following morning after sunrise, Maphuti had awoken and had begun heading towards his old Kingdom. It was at this self-same moment that Bo had begun walking on his journey to the forests to find the caterpillars – when both their paths suddenly and coincidentally crossed!

Bo had been walking at his own pace, unafraid, fearless and whistling when he bumped into Maphuti!

Both Bo and the Maphuti were completely caught off guard by this sudden and unexpected meeting in the middle of the African bush!

Both had very specific missions to accomplish. One could see the panic within each other's eyes!

Having spent years in the military, having swift reptilian-like reflexes, Maphuti was the first to react! Immediately he had Bo around his neck with the poison arrow tip pointing close to his eye. It was an impressive tactic! Bo had tried to run, but he was immediately subdued. Maphuti was as fast as an injured leopard!

"I thought we killed you!" said Bo, he was winded and short of breath.

"We watched you die! We watched the vultures eat the flesh off your bones!"

"Oh. I am very much alive!" scoffed Maphuti. *"You thought you killed me – whereas in fact you killed an old cobbler who looks like me!"*

Bo felt nausea and fear pulsate through his body. He recalled the power Maphuti had commanded. King Makohani still struck fear into his soul.

"We will go back to my cave now! Ordered Maphuti.

Bo didn't even argue. He had been conditioned. With shoulders stooped, spirit broken and mind defeated he was marched back to Maphuti's cave. The arrow tip was inches away from his back. Bo prayed that Maphuti wouldn't even poke him with it!

All Bo could think about was his Nandy, with her small pregnant belly and her soft skin and her deep penetrating eyes.

Up high in the sky, the vultures were floating off their nests, on their daily search for food.

CHAPTER 31:

THE INTERROGATION

"What were you doing walking alone so far from the Kingdom?" Demanded Maphuti.

Bo was tied to a tree just outside the cave. His wrists were tightly tied behind the tree trunk.

Maphuti whipped Bo on his abdomen with his sjambok.

"I repeat. What were you doing walking alone so far from the Kingdom?"

Bo's eyes were watering with pain. The whip of his sjambok had lacerated his skin and he was bleeding from an abdominal wound.

Maphuti whipped Bo again!

"Yo!" screamed Bo.

Maphuti whipped Bo again!

"Ai!" Screamed Bo.

"And how do you feel right now?"

"It stings!" Bo's eyes were now watering with tears.

"Tell me where you were walking!"

Maphuti raised the sjambok high above his head to whip Bo again, when suddenly Bo surrendered.

"Please no more! I will tell you where I was going!" Bo was completely submissive. He was completely oppressed, like the dog with it's tail tucked tightly between his legs. Maphuti knew how to break a person. He knew how to make a person submit.

"Go on!" Maphuti's eyes pierced Bo's eyes, *"tell me!"*

"The womenfolk from my village had found three small caterpillars in the forest near where I was born. We used the blood from the caterpillars to poison the arrow which killed Makohani! As you know, our arrow went missing and I now see that you now have our arrow. I was travelling to the forest to get some more caterpillars to make some new arrow poison."

This news was startling! Maphuti's eyes glowed and betrayed his thoughts. One could actually see his mind twisting, writhing and turning with this new information.

"You will take me to this forest!" demanded Maphuti. *"You will show me this caterpillar!"*

CHAPTER 32:

THE LONG MARCH TO THE FOREST

And so, Maphuti left with his young captive tied-up in front of him.

Bo estimated that it would take about three days for them to walk to the forest. There was no guarantee even that the caterpillars or butterflies would be found at this time of year! He remembered how hard the womenfolk from his village had searched for days and had only found three caterpillars!

Bo also had flashbacks of his cousin, the herdsboy, who had been killed by *'uvemvane !'*

He had heard stories about these poisonous butterflies from the elders as a child. He remembered how dangerous these insects could be. He remembered hearing horrific tales of villagers who died from but the gentlest of butterfly wings which had fluttered ever so lightly against them!

How the creator could create something so beautiful and so deadly was still a great mystery to Bo.

How the poison arrow tip did not seem to affect Maphuti, who was clutching it so tightly in his fist, was also a mystery to Bo. Surely the arrow poison must have dried-up or become useless with time? Still, Bo didn't want to take any chances. The arrow tip was inches away from his back. He just submitted and marched onwards.

The walk felt very uncomfortable. Not from lack of fitness, but from the uneasiness of master and servant. The power lay squarely with Maphuti. The arrow was always inches away from Bo's neck. Even when Bo needed to relieve himself, Maphuti stood over him with arrow point close-by! The situation was only made worse by Maphuti's complete lack of personality and talkativeness. Maphuti literally had nothing to say to Bo. The two men walked in silence. Even when the path seemed impenetrably overgrown, Maphuti would say nothing, he would just gesture and grunt for Bo to lead the way.

The leather ropes surrounding Bo's ankles made it impossible for him to run. All Bo could do was shuffle at a relatively brisk pace.

At night, Bo was tied to a nearby tree while Maphuti made a fire and scavenged for something to eat. Bo was given minimal food and water, just enough to keep going the next day. Maphuti realized that he no longer needed Bo once he had the caterpillars. The plan in Maphuti's mind was to kill Bo as soon as Bo located the butterfly and/or caterpillars.

CHAPTER 33:

THE THUNDERSTORM

The day had started off like any other. The early morning was fresh and crisp in the African bush. The birds were chirping and there was still some dew on the grasses.

Maphuti and Bo had awoken early. Bo knew that there was a long walk ahead of them that day. He realized that they would have to walk a great distance across the open savannah grasslands towards the forest streams. There were some signs late morning that it was going to be a very hot day for them.

By late morning, the day was fully upon them. They had both been walking consistently and they were both very tired.

By noon, the sun was at its highest and the heat poured down from the sky. Both Bo and Maphuti were sweating greatly. There was no water to be found except for their two small calabashes between them.

'Please can we rest!' Begged Bo.

'Yes!' said Maphuti, *'We will rest under that tree!'* He was clearly also being affected by the heat.

There was one single umbrella tree, growing all alone, in the middle of the vast grasslands.

The two men sat quietly under the large umbrella tree in the middle of the African grasslands. It was a beautiful and picturesque setting. The silence around them was deafening. One single acacia tree growing alone in the middle of nowhere! There was only one lone surviving tree in a vast ocean of grassland. Obviously, it was deposited there many years ago by an elephant. Elephants were known to walk great distances and obviously the acacia seed must have arrived there via elephant dung, for there were no other acacia trees to be seen from horizon to horizon! It was just endless grass plains for as far as the eyes could see.

Maphuti tied Bo's wrists to the tree trunk behind his back with leather rope. In the distance there were herds of impala grazing. The sun was white-hot and the tree provided both men with adequate shade.

'How much further do we have to walk?' Grunted Maphuti.

'The mountains and the forests are at the edge of these grasslands. We are nearly there,' answered Bo.

'I am going to get some sleep!' grunted Maphuti, *'We will continue walking later, when the heat cools down!'*

Bo was also tired. The walking with leather ropes around his ankles had tired him. He was burned by the sun and he was thirsty. He felt depressed and resigned himself to his situation. He sat limp against the tree trunk. Wrists tied tightly behind his back. It was not long before he too blacked-out from tiredness.

By the time both men awoke, late afternoon, a thunderstorm had crept up on them. The warm winds and the deep, rolling thunder, were the first things to awaken them from their afternoon slumber.

Few things can compete with the raw beauty and devastating power of a raging African thunderstorm.

Bo was still tied to the tree. A mighty flash of lightning suddenly cracked in the distance. Maphuti was startled by this. He gazed at the horizon. He still couldn't see mountains or forests. The sky had taken on a dark-grey colour. Their only cover from the storm would be that single acacia tree! The wind was blowing harder. There was the distant smell of rain upon the wind. Another crack of lightning pierced the air.

'We will wait under this tree until the storm passes!' shouted Maphuti, because the wind speed had picked up significantly.

'Please untie my hands. We are both in this situation together!' pleaded Bo

Single, large raindrops began to pelt down on both men. The suddenness of the storm had caught them both unawares. The raindrops stung Bo's skin. Maphuti sat opposite Bo, on the opposite side of the tree trunk, where he was somewhat more protected than Bo from the rain. The sky was dark and menacing and it wasn't even night.

'Okay, I will untie you! But do not try and escape!'

In the beginning there was silence and darkness and then came more warm wind and another flash from the sky. Thunder and lightning kept crashing down around the two men, hitting the earth and splitting the ground, like a fire burning high in the sky.

Bo suddenly felt a burning sensation down his back. There was a loud noise. It was almost as if everything was lit up around him. Afterwards, everything else was left in darkness and it was suddenly quiet.

It happened as soon as Maphuti had finished untying Bo's hands. It happened suddenly and without warning. It was unfortunate that the two men had taken shelter under that lonesome tree, for there simply was nowhere else to seek shelter. Some of the bark exploded and wooden chips were thrown far away. The lightning had hit the tallest object and both men died instantaneously. Both lives extinguished in a single flash.

It was as sudden and as senseless as that.

The tiny little drafts of air caused by the butterfly's wings all those months before had ultimately affected the weather. Such a seemingly insignificant event did have a consequence. The insignificant little wing beats had caused their ultimate death. Yet the consequences were not finished yet...

CHAPTER 34:

PROFESSOR SUTCLIFFE

Professor Sutcliffe had created the perfect 'butterfly brew'. His brew attracted butterflies from far and wide! Basically, it consisted of 8 overripe bananas, one cup of brown cane sugar, one bottle of dark beer, a drop of vanilla essence – and his secret ingredient: leopard dung! This mixture drove butterflies' wild! He had blended the mixture together a couple of days beforehand and was now walking with his butterfly brew through the dark forest floor. The 'funk' of his brew was overwhelming, yet in this remote forested region, only he and his two students could thoroughly appreciate it.

He and his two post-graduate students were posted to the Kakamega forest region in Kenya to catalogue the regional butterflies. The butterflies of central-eastern Africa were a complete mystery to the scientific world due to years of conflict in the region, and had only recently opened up due to a very amenable new governing party. The fermenting, sweet brew had already attracted approximately twenty or thirty tropical butterflies, which were fluttering wildly around them as they walked through the humid jungle.

Sutcliffe's massive Nikon camera dangled precariously over his right shoulder. He was a fanatic and extremist in every sense of the word! He was a militaristic conservationist. He hated people and liked best to be alone in some forest or jungle with his birds, his insects and most of all – his butterflies!

Sutcliffe was a loner and had never married. He did have one son in his twenties, Theo, with whom he had minimal contact. He led a military existence. He would typically wake up at 3am. He would do 100 sit-ups, 100 push-ups and 100 squats. Then he would eat a 'deconstructed' salad consisting of tomatoes, lettuce and cucumber. He also loved his dried meats and his cheeses!

Sutcliffe was a coffee snob. He would only drink the finest coffee. He shunned instant coffee! No matter where he found himself on the planet, he would always brew his own perfect blend and take his coffee plunger with him. He also only drank his coffee with coconut cream, which he carried with him in its own hermetically-sealed container.

Sutcliffe had published five textbooks on butterflies from all over the world. He had a huge following on social websites and was considered the 'guru' at nature fairs! He had a huge following and every entomological and Lepidoptera student knew his name. He had caught butterflies in almost every tropical habitat in the world. More importantly he had re-discovered six 'extinct' species of butterfly and he had no less than three species named after him!

He had published widely and funding opportunities were never a problem for him. He was often sponsored by multi-nationals to go on expeditions to find this or that species. He merely had to ask and his reputation was so fierce that he would be granted his funds. He was also often consulted to do environmental impact assessments.

Oftentimes his butterflying would take him into hostile territories. He had caught butterflies in the middle of war zones. He had nearly been arrested several times and he had more than one type of weapon shoved in his face or back. This was another reason he hated humans so much. Humans always seemed to be around and they were generally troublesome!

His dry sense of humour and his habits made him seem somewhat eccentric to laymen. For example, he always wore a hat, not just any old hat, his hat was truly unique. It was a floppy leather hat with a huge Bird of Paradise feather protruding from its side!

His leather belt also was packed with a multitude of pouches and holsters containing everything from knives to tweezers to pepper spray. His vest was also unique in that it had many pockets, also containing a multitude of strange paraphernalia.

One of his favourite sayings was: *'Because none of this makes any sense – we do what we do!'*

He was much loved by all of his students and if anyone embodied true happiness it was him. He understood that happiness cannot be travelled to, owned, earned, worn or consumed. To Sutcliffe, happiness was simply the experience of living every minute with mindfulness and gratitude.

Accompanying Sutcliffe was two of his students. Both were doing their Masters degrees in tropical insect studies. The girl was blonde, fairly attractive in her late twenties, her name was Sarah Carrington. She was quite head-strong. The other was a Sri-Lankan boy, also in his late twenties, named Raj Makurai. Both were excellent students, very attentive and thus far proved to be excellent travel companions for the Professor.

Sarah was incredibly athletic, and wore the latest in hiking and sports gear. She was the kind of girl who entered triathlons and trail running and mountain biking races. Always busy with physical training in her spare time. She lived alone and from what Professor Sutcliffe could gather, her dad was extremely wealthy and somewhat influential. Her mother apparently died from breast cancer. She actually didn't need to study, yet she was studying entomology in his Department out of sheer passion. She apparently had a genuine love for insects! She had quite a collection of spiders and stick insects in her apartment. As far as Prof Sutcliffe knew, she didn't have a boyfriend. He could suppose that she must have seemed too eccentric and scary for most of the boys she knew!

Raj on the other hand was a quiet boy, very gentle, very kind and very non-confrontational. He almost seemed 'spiritual'. He would usually hang out at the back of their expedition, moving to the beat of his own drum, which seemed to be a relatively slow beat! He was incredibly curious and would often stop and examine a flower or a moss or a lichen, whilst Prof and Sarah were quite far ahead. Raj spoke very little, but when he did it was quite authoritative and seemed to come from a place deep within his heart.

They had all stopped in a small opening in the middle of the forest. This was an incredibly rare opportunity as the forest was so incredible dense, oppressive, gloomy and somewhat depressing.

'We will set-up our traps here!' decided the Professor.

Sutcliffe's butterfly bait traps had a number of features designed to improve performance and ease of use. There was a square landing platform made of easy to clean semi-rigid PVC. The bait or bait dish was placed on top of this. Support cords attached the main trap cylinder to the landing platform. The main netting cylinder was fully washable and was sewn with no internal projecting seams. A double-top loop provided a secure hanging point. The cylinder was fitted with a full length double-slider side zip, for easy access to the butterflies at any point, and for the removal of unwanted insects. The larger trap also featured an integral cone, to minimise butterfly escape. The white netting helped to encourage butterflies towards the upper end of the trap.

'Let's settle down and have some lunch! I'm feeling a bit snackish!' said Sutcliffe.

The three sat down on the buttress of large green fig tree and Sutcliffe began the ritual of making himself some good plunger coffee. He also took out some cheese and dried meats and between the three of them they settled down to a hearty lunch in the middle of the forest. Despite the humidity and the buzzing of the cicadas, the sounds of birds and other insects all around them made this a very memorable moment indeed!

After about half-an-hour Sutcliffe said that he would like to go and examine his traps.

Fluttering awkwardly within the white net was the strangest butterfly Sutcliffe had ever seen! Its beauty was unparalleled. Its majestic colours hypnotized all three onlookers. Its wings erupted violently in the most brilliant primary colours, all meticulously arranged in a swirl and a whirl next to one another! Each of the extreme primary colours was neatly arranged next to one another.

Mesmerized, Sutcliffe carefully opened the trap. One of the butterfly wings twitched and fluttered ever so lightly against his hand. Sutcliffe usually avoided touching the wing surfaces with his fingers which would rub off the scales. Sutcliffe ignored the fluttering and quickly pinched its thorax (middle body segment) between his thumb and forefinger. This technique had taken some practice to learn the proper pressure, but stunned the specimen was immediately prevented from damaging itself.

The stunned specimen was then quickly slid into an envelope, with its wings over its back. Butterfly specimens can be kept in this condition indefinitely in a box with moth balls or other insecticide to protect the specimen from damage by dermestid beetle larvae and book lice, until they are ready for mounting.

Sutcliffe called Raj to come take a closer look at the specimen. He grabbed Raj by the forearm with the same hand he had used to pinch the thorax of the butterfly. Scales from the butterfly wings were also transferred to Raj's forearm.

The first symptom was hypersalivation. Both Sutcliffe and Raj noticed increased watery saliva production. Sutcliffe's right hand was beginning to itch. Raj's forearm also began to itch.

Both men suddenly became light-headed. Their drooling increased. Within a short space of time both men became dizzy, nauseous and weak. Even before Sutcliffe could ask Sarah for water to wash his hand, Sutcliffe collapsed face down in the forest. His body didn't even shake or twitch.

Seconds later, Raj also collapsed next to the forest floor.

Within a period of moments, Sarah found herself alone in the forested jungles of Central-Eastern Africa. Her mentor and her closest friend - dead.

CHAPTER 35:

SARAH CARRINGTON

The forest was dark and dank and deep and seemed to close in around her. Sarah was having a panic attack and felt claustrophobic. She felt nauseous and alone. She had quickly realized what had happened. Obviously the butterfly had somehow killed Professor and Raj. She checked their pulses. Both bodies were lifeless. Both bodies felt warm and flaccid. Sarah checked her emotions. This was no time to have a nervous breakdown. She had to get out the forest. She had to alert the authorities. She had to manage this situation.

Immediately she gathered her possessions. Immediately she switched on the satellite navigation phone. It would take her about three hours to find her way out of the forest. It would take her a further three hours to get to her hotel.

Her mind was overwhelmed with thoughts. What would the authorities say? Would she be arrested? Would she be detained? How was she going to get home? Her passport and papers were with Prof Sutcliffe. How would she break the news to her folks? How would she break the news to the University? And who would break the news to Raj's parents?

She felt completely and utterly devastated. She gathered her few possessions and a few of her Prof's possessions. She carefully placed the dead butterfly and sealed it in an envelope. She was extremely careful not to touch it! She placed the envelope in her rucksack.

She left the bodies *in situ.* And she began her purposeful walk out of the forest. Suddenly the forest seemed very scary alone. There were stinging nettles in the forest and Safari ants – both which caused pain! Sarah walked purposefully and carefully with her hands in her pockets.

The swift walking managed to keep her mind focussed. Sarah hacked and bashed her way through some of the jungle path. Luckily she didn't get lost. She had a brilliant memory and could remember distinctly the route they had used to get to where they were. She was also skilled with the satellite navigation GPS.

Three hours later, Sarah emerged sweaty and distraught at the forest edge. She immediately tried to wave down one of the locals on the district road.

Driving slowly up the district road was a young black man on a noisy, low-budget, motorcycle.

'Please take me to the President Hotel!' She implored the young man who was riding the low-budget motorcycle.

The man immediately nodded, he understood the terms *'President Hotel'* and she climbed on the back of the bike and grabbed him tightly around his waist. She began to sob as they puttered slowly up the hill.

CHAPTER 36:

THE PRESIDENT HOTEL

Sarah arrived back at the President hotel in Nairobi. She felt physically and emotionally exhausted. She didn't quite know where to begin. The first thing she did was phone her dad back in South Africa.

The phone rang once and immediately her father answered.

"Daddy! Prof Sutcliffe and Raj are dead! They died in the forest!" She sobbed and could hardly contain her emotions which overflowed.

"Relax my Girl!" tell me what happened.

"I don't know what exactly happened! We were catching butterflies and I think they were stung or something! But both Prof and Raj are now dead! They are still lying in the forest. I'm all alone here. What must I do?" Sarah pleaded desperately.

"I will phone you back in five minutes! Wait by your phone!" her dad put her at ease.

Sarah sat rocking on her bed in the hotel. Phone clutched tightly in her sweaty hand. The five minutes felt like forever! Her mind was racing. She was still drenched in dried sweat.

Five minutes later the phone rang.

"Hi daddy?" Sarah said.

"Hi my Girl, listen I want you to go to the South African Embassy and tell them what happened. You understand? You need to speak to the officials there."

"Daddy, its already 17h00 here. The embassy will be closed. I will have to go first thing tomorrow morning!"

"Okay. But please lock your hotel door and don't go out tonight. You will need to manage this with a clear head first thing tomorrow morning. I'll try and get hold of the officials on this side and start the ball rolling. Tomorrow morning you must head out straight to the embassy!"

Sarah's dad, Norman Carrington, had served in the South African Navy for many years and was now retired. He was old-school military-minded. Trained in Naval etiquette he was cut from the original cloth. He stood when a woman stood. He ate at the same pace as his guests. He passed the salt correctly. He spoke appropriately. He drank correctly. He was well-mannered. He knew how to dress-up. He knew how to speak-up. He was respected by all his peers. He was a gentleman's gentleman.

Nairobi was chaos. The traffic was mad. Luckily the South African Embassy was only four blocks away from her hotel. Sarah packed her bag and stuffed the envelope containing the dead butterfly into one of the side pockets. She drank some water and took a shower. She stripped off her sweaty clothes and threw them in a plastic bag. She tried to compose herself.

After her shower, while blow-drying her hair, she heard a knock on her hotel room door.

"One minute!" she said, as she quickly put on some clean denims and a white t-shirt.

Sarah opened the door to find three big Kenyan policemen standing at the door!

"Miss Carrington?"

"Yes." She replied timidly.

"We are arresting you for the murders of Professor Nigel Sutcliff and Mr Raj Makurai!"

Sarah was stunned. She was shocked. She said nothing.

With that, they slapped a pair of tight-fitting, rusted handcuffs on her petite little wrists.

Sarah was then escorted to Kamiti prison in Nairobi.

CHAPTER 37:

KAMITI PRISON

The first thing that struck Sarah was the smell. She was placed into a holding cell with another woman. There was a very primitive toilet and wash basin in the one corner. The walls had graffiti written all over it. There were no windows. It was a pure, cold, concrete holding cell. There weren't even beds. The only view was of the corridor through a barred, locked front gate.

The background sounds were also terrifying. It was loud. She couldn't see other prisoners, yet she could hear them. Her prison mate was a large African female of approximately 120 kg. She had an expressionless face as she sat mutely and stared at Sarah as she entered the holding cell.

The barred prison door slammed loudly behind her as she was roughly thrown inside the cell. The ride to the prison was very unpleasant. Despite her constant pleading with the Kenyan police officials, they were all dead silent and they did not engage her. They had simply stone-walled her. She seemed to have no rights at all. There was nothing she could do or say.

Sarah was informed that the young man who was riding the low-budget motorcycle had informed the police. Apparently, there was a lot of human traffic passing through the Kakamega forest. It was not as wild and untouched as Sarah believed. In fact, the bodies were discovered and reported to the police before Sarah even returned to her hotel!

According to the Kenyan police, post mortem examinations were to be performed on the bodies the first thing the following morning! Sarah couldn't believe the efficiency of the police system in this remote African region! Although deeply terrified, she was secretly impressed with the authorities' effectiveness!

The large black woman didn't even greet Sarah upon her entry into the cell. Sarah went and sat as far away from her cell-mate as possible. She tried to be friendly and make eye contact, but her cell mate made no effort – not even an eyebrow flash. Sarah felt scared and she could feel the adrenaline pumping through her body.

As soon as the door shut and the large iron keys clanked, the big black woman stood up and walked purposefully towards Sarah. Sarah swallowed nervously and stood her ground.

The large black woman said nothing. She just went up to Sarah and hugged her tight. Very tight! In a bear-like grip! She wouldn't let her go. Sarah went completely passive. She didn't resist. She didn't fight. She just allowed herself to be held by this very large woman. Both fell to the floor. And that is how she spent the entire night, in the Kamiti prison, being held, tightly, by this large, mute, African woman.

CHAPTER 38:

THE NEXT MORNING

The following morning, the police came to fetch Sarah from the holding cell. She was completely invisible at first. The large black woman was lying over her, completely engulfing her small little body. Only Sarah's face was exposed, eyes wide open, trying to breathe air. Her mouth was next to her captor's ear. Sarah hadn't slept the entire night. She hadn't even gone to the toilet!

A large male Kenyan police official entered the holding cell and screamed at the large African Woman:

'Let her go Mampi!'

Yet Mampi refused to let Sarah go. In fact, she hugged Sarah tighter, almost squeezing the air out of her!

'Mampi! Let her go!' Another larger male police official entered the holding cell with a baton.

Mampi refused to let Sarah go. The second police official lifted his baton high up in the air and swung it down sharply onto Mampi's buttocks. Sarah could feel the force of the blow transmitted through Mampi's fat. Mampi then squeezed Sarah even harder. There was another blow to Mampi's body. Sarah could hardly breathe! She felt like a rag doll being clutched in the vice of a dumb child.

Suddenly another large male police official entered the room. He too had a baton.

'Let her go Mampi!'

Mampi refused. The officer took his baton and rapped it against the bars of the prison door. The baton made a clunk-clunk-clunk sound.

The two large police officials suddenly started beating Mampi with their batons. It was violent.

The third police official dragged Sarah from the clutches of Mampi.

Sarah caught a brief glimpse of sadness and simpleness within Mampi's eyes. She felt relieved and at the same time, incredibly sorry for her. The police continued to beat Mampi while Sarah was escorted out of the holding cell towards the reception area. The entire time, Mampi didn't even cry or scream or make any sounds whatsoever. Just the rhythmic sound of the batons slapping against her fat flesh is all Sarah could hear. And then the loud clank of the large iron door.

Waiting in the reception area was Mrs Janse van Rensburg, the South African Diplomat to Kenya. For the first time since the deaths of Prof Sutcliffe and Raj, Sarah broke down in tears.

Mrs Janse van Rensburg went up to the young blonde girl and gave her a hug. The last thing Sarah Carrington needed was another hug! Yet she gracefully accepted it and sobbed uncontrollably.

CHAPTER 39:

THE ROUTINE

What saves you in life is your routine. Your routine is what keeps you alive when you don't have the motivation or energy to decide for yourself. In the elderly, the ones who thrive are the ones who have the best routines.

Routines come from years and years of habit. For example, if every Wednesday evening you meet with your friends for coffee, then Wednesday evenings are taken care of. If every Saturday morning you play chess, then Saturday mornings are taken care of. This is the great thing about routines. Once they are firmly established they tend to keep you going.

Luckily Sarah already had a good routine to come home to. Sarah would have her dinner club every Tuesday night with her female friends. Sarah would also volunteer at the local zoological gardens every Saturday morning. She also used to attend a yoga class twice a week and a cooking class once a month. It was these little routines which helped Sarah re-integrate herself back into society and normality.

Very soon Sarah realized that she had very little control over what happened in her life. She realized that there were no guarantees in life. So she rooted herself in the moment. She had a lot of time to contemplate things. She managed to reflect on what had happened to her in Kenya. She realized that she had stoically accepted everything without complaint. Even her friends and family were remarkably surprised as to how resilient she was.

She had known Professor Sutcliffe and Raj Makurai for about three years. The quality time she had spent with them could never be taken away from her. She would often think back to the good times (and bad times!) she had had with them. Their sudden unexpected deaths still sat uncomfortably with her.

Approximately two months later, Sarah was summoned to the Kenyan embassy in Pretoria. Apparently Mrs Janse van Rensburg, the South African Diplomat to Kenya, was there with the autopsy reports of Professor Sutcliffe and Raj Makurai. Sarah's dad, Norman, was also present.

"Good day Miss Carrington, good day Mr Carrington and good day Mrs van Rensburg. *Jambo to you all!*" The large Kenyan official greeted Sarah warmly as she stepped into the large meeting room. He had a large, wide, open face. He seemed friendly and had perfect teeth. His name was Mr Wairimu.

Gentleman that he was, Norman Carrington pulled out the seats for the ladies and allowed them to be seated first.

Everyone sat down around a large glass table and an assistant came in and offered everyone some original Kenyan tea. The room was filled with a rich, strong, steaming tea aroma.

"*As you folks are aware,*" he began. "*We have received the autopsy reports and toxicology results from the Kenyan officials, regarding the unnatural deaths of Professor Sutcliffe and Raj Makurai.* "

Sarah watched Mr Wairimu with mixed emotions. She didn't know if the news was going to be good or bad. Mrs van Rensburg was also very guarded with her emotions. Norman grabbed his daughter's hand very firmly under the table.

"*Both victims autopsy reports and both victims toxicology reports came to the same conclusion with respect to cause of death. Both victims seemed to have died unexpectedly and suddenly. The precise terminal* causes of death were deemed to be unascertainable at autopsy examination alone"

"The Kenyan authorities are happy to close this matter. We are just sorry that we don't have a formal cause of death for you folks."

"It was the butterfly!" remarked Sarah. "Both Prof and both Raj touched a butterfly which had been trapped in the net!"

"Butterflies can't kill you!" exclaimed Mr Wairimu, in a somewhat incredulous tone.

"Look, the Kenyan Police have ruled out foul-play in this regard and as far as we are concerned, these were both natural deaths and this matter is now closed." Mr Waimiru continued.

"Furthermore, on behalf of the Kenyan Government, we would sincerely like to apologize for arresting and detaining Miss Carrington in prison during this ordeal. We believe that this was a wrongful arrest on our part and we, as the Kenyan Government, would like to pay some sort of compensation or restitution for her suffering". Mr Waimiru looked squarely at Mrs Janse van Rensburg, the South African Diplomat, in this regard. "I am sure we can work something out?"

"Thank you very much for the kind offer!" responded Mrs van Rensburg. "We too are extremely happy that this whole matter is over." She looked straight at Sarah, making strong eye-contact, and then she shifted her gaze towards Sarah's dad also giving him a look suggesting that they all accept this result.

Mrs Janse van Rensberg continued, "I think that we would gladly accept whatever offer you propose, miss Carrington did suffer greatly through this ordeal and I am sure that she would accept whatever gift you folks are offering? Wouldn't you Sarah?"

Sarah sat uncomfortably in her chair and shifted around restlessly, she knew that this was not the truth. She knew that both Prof and Raj were exposed to some sort of toxin. Probably the Kenyan medico-legal system wasn't technologically advanced enough to detect the toxin? Sarah thought to herself that this was just the way it was. It was just another theory in the world which would be impossible to prove.

Sarah cleared her throat, took a thoughtful sip of her tea, looked at her dad and slowly responded: *"Thank you Mr Waimiru, thank you for this meeting, thank you for communicating with us, I am happy that this ordeal is over. I just want to get home and continue with my life. I lost a great mentor and a great friend in this ordeal"*.

"Sarah, the Kenyan government is prepared to offer you and your father a two-week holiday in Kenya at one of its finest resorts in compensation for your loss and suffering. How does that sound?" Mr Waimiru beamed with this news.

Sarah didn't want to go back to Kenya *ever again* after her experience! Now she was offered this extremely kind gift. Sarah looked at her dad and she looked at Mrs Janse van Rensberg.

"Okay, we accept!" She said. She didn't know where her answer came from.

CHAPTER 40:

BACK TO KENYA

Sarah and her dad arrived in Kenya later that year. They were to be staying at a new five-star lodge in the Masai Mara reserve.

Sarah and her dad were picked up at the Kenyan international airport and chauffeured all the way to the Mara. Their chauffer's name was Patrick and he was quite a friendly fellow. Patrick was to transfer them from the airport to the lodge. Their car was a 4 x 4 land-cruiser of the open canopy rooftop variety, which could be adjusted to the raised-up or closed-down position. The car was very comfortable and there was an air conditioner. It was hot and humid this time of year, for they were very close to the equator.

Sarah was looking good. She had her strong positive attitude back. She was fit and seemed to have her old bravado. Her dad was quiet and content and he was just happy to spend some quality time with his daughter. Sarah's mother had died of breast cancer about five years back and now it was just the two of them.

Sarah was beautiful by any man's standards. She had the heart-aching-type of beauty that would make any man weak at his knees. Her eyes were dark brown. Her hair was perfectly straight and now dyed brown. She had the build of an athlete - Legs like a runner, the abdomen of a swimmer, and breasts like a ballerina. She definitely had a presence about herself. She could walk on a high-end fashion runway or disappear amongst the masses dressed in a tracksuit. Her beauty was that versatile! She hated makeup and perfume. By all accounts, Sarah Carrington was a natural beauty.

She was definitely her dad's girl. She was tough and a real tomboy. Besides her dad, she didn't need a man in her life. She even used to tell her female friends that she would one day go to a sperm-bank if she wanted to fall pregnant! She simply saw no purpose for men! As far as Sarah was concerned, she could do quite well without them! If she needed an item from the top shelf, she could use a step-ladder. If she needed to open a tight jar, she had a special machine for that. Sarah Carrington was completely self-reliant and self-sufficient. She never had a boyfriend. She never wanted one and she saw no purpose for relationships.

The road to the Masai Mara was very bad. The corrugations on the road were like waves at places, and Sarah and her dad were tossed- and bumped around on the back seat. Apparently, there was no desire to tar the road to the Mara, because the locals believed that it would destroy the allure of the Masai Mara. The locals certainly didn't want tourists self-driving their own little 'smart cars' in the mighty Masai Mara to view their animals. No matter how good it would be for their economy!

There were lots of animals on the road, chiefly domestic animals like donkeys, cattle, goats and chickens – like most places in Africa. The Wildebeest migration had taken place in August and there were still some Wildebeest loitering on the loitre-plains, surrounding the Masai Mara nature reserve.

The road was getting worse. At places the road seemed to almost disappear before them! Yet, despite this, Patrick remained unperturbed and carried on chauffeuring them to their lodge. This was 'normal' driving conditions for Patrick. In the background, the song 'Paradise Road' by Joy was playing on the radio. Sarah's dad commented to

Sarah that he thought this song was ironic, because there were burning bridges behind them, fire was smoking and the sky was blazing. Sarah just scoffed as her dad and said that he mustn't be so cynical!

Within about 6 hours after they touched down at Nairobi International Airport, they finally arrived at their lodge.

Patrick turned around for the first time the entire trip and made strong eye contact with both of them. He smiled. He had perfect teeth.

"Welcome to the *King Makohani mountain top lodge!*"

CHAPTER 41:

THE KING MAKOHANI MOUNTAIN-TOP LODGE

Apparently, over 300 men worked day and night, winter and summer, for 13 months to complete this luxurious game lodge. The lodge was owned by Sir Arthur Madock - the eccentric Irish Billionaire who had purchased the property and developed it into a world-class, five-star mountain-top lodge. Madock-owned eccentric 'off-the-grid' five star resorts all over the world. This was one of *Madock Luxury Lodges'* first and premier projects. He had purchased the land from the local Manyuki tribe.

The paving was hacked into the mountainside, passing through five tunnels to get to the entrance of the lodge. Heavy wooden gates heralded the opening to Makohani's mountain-top lodge, which was located on the summit, and which gave a grand view of all the surrounding vast grasslands and Savannah plains.

Such a marvel of architecture was unheard of in this time. Apparently, the summit was the heart of an ancient Kingdom and the lodge was named after a King - King Makohani.

"Surely he must have been a great visionary in order to locate such a magnificent site!" Mused Norman.

The paving towards the summit appeared perfectly manicured. The detail of the foot stones blew Sarah and her dad away. Each stone had unique and ornate markings - and there were thousands of them! Each stone was designed, handcrafted and laid by hand. Such craftsmanship, Sarah's dad had only seen in a few old European villages.

The 4 x 4 land-cruiser crawled slowly up the paving towards the top of the mountain. When Sarah looked down, the height was dizzying!

'Look!' said Sarah, pointing to several Cape Griffon vultures, which were nesting on the nearby cliffs and which were up soaring in the air.

The entire time, Patrick focussed on the road. He was not very talkative. He answered the few questions they had very briefly and concentrated on the road. *And rightly so*, because one mistake and they would all end up on the bottom of these cliffs!

It was late afternoon when they finally arrived at the lodge and they were welcomed by four cheerful staff members with welcoming drinks. The landscaping and the garden of the lodge were breath taking. Sarah and her dad were handed cocktails made from the local Maroela trees. They were also given warm towels to wipe their faces and necks.

'Welcome To the King Makohani Mountain-Top Lodge! Please come to the reception' said a friendly young black female.

'I will bring your luggage', said Patrick.

The air atop the mountain was so crisp and so fresh that both Sarah and her dad felt light-headed – or was it the alcohol in the Maroela drinks.

Sitting at the reception was a young white man, probably in his early forties. His name, as they were to find out, was Rowan - Rowan Madock - the only son of the Irish billionaire who owned the luxury lodge franchise. Rowan managed the lodge.

Rowan had red hair, freckles, he was tall and well-built. He had blue eyes and a confident air about himself. The way he introduced himself was with his energy. Before he even said anything, you could feel his energy. It was a restless kind of energy. The kind of energy one finds in travellers and those who chase things – even when the earth sleeps.

Rowan was immediately attracted to Sarah! Here was an immaculately dressed and professional young playboy, clearly dispatched by his dad to learn the trade. However at the sight of Sarah, he seemed to lose a bit of composure! The only thing which seemed to keep him in check was Sarah's dad!

'Welcome to Makohani Mountain-Top Lodge Folks!' Rowan beamed.

'How was your trip up here from the airport? It's a bit of a bumpy road hey?'

Norman responded: *'It has been a long day driving and we are somewhat tired. We would love to check in to our room. What time does dinner get served and where is the venue?'*

Rowan immediately and professionally responded: *'You folks will be staying in the Acacia suite – our finest suite - and dinner will be served at 19h00 on the terrace. We have an infinity pool on our wooden deck which overlooks the plains below. We think you folks will enjoy the view!'*

Norman and Sarah retired to their large room. The room was truly magnificent. How the builders had managed to build such luxury on the top of a remote mountain, in the middle of Africa, really astounded them both. The finest fittings were present in the bathroom. In fact, the bathroom looked like something out of colonial Africa! The finest touches were present within their room – from the carpet décor to the paintings on the walls. Both Sarah and her dad stood there, soaking in the details, before they even unpacked and settled down.

At 19h00, dressed in their evening clothes, both Sarah and her dad arrived on the terrace. It was past sunset and the grasslands extended endlessly in all directions, with colours of tan and apricot and orange.

There were three tables with families (including kids), two tables with couples and a single table with a black man who was dressed in an incredibly smart suit. It was really exclusive and clearly attracted only the wealthiest of clients. Sarah looked at the clothes and watches and jewellery of the other guests. This was obviously a secret destination for the unabashedly fortunate!

Sarah and her dad sat down near the balcony close to the pool, away from the other guests. Their waiter, Sam arrived, extremely well-dressed and incredibly well spoken he beamed perfect white teeth and welcomed them both to the lodge and ran through the specials of the evening.

Apparently the lodge chef qualified at the legendary *École de Cuisine Alain Ducasse*. She was apparently highly skilled in African cuisine and apparently added a 'French twist' to the many local African culinary dishes.

Norman ordered the grilled springbok loin with hummus, sautéed chickpeas, broccoli, potato fondant, marrow croquette and bordelaise jus.

Sarah ordered the grilled sea bass with pea purée, confit parsnips, sautéed peas, polenta duchesse, fresh parsnip shavings, bacon crumble and lemon butter sauce.

The meal was excellent! While they were sitting in the aftermath of the dinner, enjoying their dessert, Rowan came past their table.

"How was dinner folks?"

"It was an excellent meal!" Replied Norman, while sipping on his Dom Pedro.

Sarah still made little eye contact with Rowan. She could sense that he liked her. The conversation and the energy drifted between Rowan and Norman and Sarah just sat there, indifferent, gazing out on the horizon, also sipping her Dom Pedro cocktail. She clearly had no interest in this young man who looked like an older version of Ron Weasley from Harry Potter.

'We have arranged a luxury game-drive for you folks tomorrow with our drivers Roebuck and Timothy. They truly are excellent guides –the best of the best! - I am sure

you folks will see the Big-5 in one morning: Lion, elephant, Buffalo, rhinocerous and even leopard!"

"What is more, we have arranged a luxury bush breakfast for you folks somewhere in the wilderness. Wake-up will be at 6 am sharp. Also we will have coffees and teas for you before you depart. Please take some sunscreen and a hat. Also perhaps take some mosquito repellent"

"That sound quite nice, doesn't it Sarah?" Norman tried to engage Sarah into the conversation.

"Yes, it does sound quite nice." Sarah responded flatly, ignoring them both, as she sipped on her Dom Pedro.

Rowan gave them both a charming smile and wished them both a good night and swiftly departed.

The stars in the sky were three-dimensional that night. There was not an artificial light glowing on the horizon, except for the brief white flash of distant lightning from a very distant thunderstorm. The air was fresh and crisp. And from the plains below one could almost hear the wails of a hyena and the cry of a jackal.

CHAPTER 42:

THE GAME DRIVE

There was a large umbrella tree in the middle of the African grasslands. It was a beautiful and picturesque setting. The silence around them was deafening. One single acacia tree growing alone in the middle of nowhere! This was the only lone surviving tree in a vast ocean of grassland. Obviously, it was deposited there many years ago by an elephant. Elephants were known to walk great distances and obviously the acacia seed must have arrived there via elephant dung, for there were no other acacia trees to be seen from horizon to horizon! It was just endless grass plains for as far as the eyes could see.

The game vehicle stopped next to the tree. It was 09h15 in the morning. It was already starting to get hot. Already, in the distance, one could see small specks of vultures soaring on the thermals. Sarah and her dad alighted from the game vehicle. The tour guide and the game tracker also alighted from the vehicle. It had been an excellent morning game drive! They had already seen good leopard and lion and it was now time for a hearty African breakfast.

Roebuck, the chief safari guide and driver instructed Timothy, the game tracker, to remove the cooler box and the table from the back of the vehicle. Timothy covered the collapsible steel table with a perfect chequered tablecloth. He pulled out a vacuum flask with piping hot Kenyan coffee and there were some African breads and cheeses upon it, which they snacked upon. It was the perfect morning in Africa! Everything felt so colonial! The freshest breeze with the purest of savannah grassland air filled their nostrils. Sarah hugged her dad tightly as they both sipped their coffee.

Roebuck was particularly chirpy this morning. He was regaling his two guests with stories of death and adventure in Africa! He was very well-spoken and Sarah's dad could see why he was hired to be the chief tour guide at King Makohani's five-star guest lodge.

"This tree," began Roebuck in a very dramatic fashion, patting the tree with his right hand.

"This umbrella acacia tree is over three hundred years old!"

Sarah and her dad approached the tree and took a closer look at the bark.

"You can clearly see where the animals have used this as a scratching post for over three hundred years." Roebuck ran his hand over the incredibly smooth and polished wood bark.

"That old mark on the bark was probably caused by lightning." He pointed higher up where some of the bark appeared chipped.

Sarah looked as Roebuck and asked: *"How come there is only one tree in all these parts? How come only this lone tree survives?"*

Timothy stood a way from the three. He was scanning the horizon for dangerous animals, AK-47 rifle on his shoulder. He had professionally distanced himself from the conversation. His duty was to protect the guests.

"Traditional plant use is of tremendous importance in rural African communities. This knowledge is dwindling due to changes towards a more Western lifestyle, and the influence of modern tourism." Roebuck said.

"Plants have been an integral part of life in many indigenous communities, and African communities are no exception. Apart from providing building materials, fodder, weapons and other commodities, plants are

especially important as traditional medicines. Since this knowledge is still mostly taught orally, without written record, the loss of knowledge is accelerating."

"Timothy and I are members of the Manyuki tribe. We were originally nomadic pastoralists. We originally lived on the shores of a great lake below the Mahale Mountain range. Our women would walk into the surrounding forests by day collecting fruits and nuts and we men would go out and catch bush meat. Bush meat consisted chiefly of primates; although bushbuck and bush pig were also often caught. When we weren't in the forests, both men and women would be out on the vast lake catching fish.

"The main pillars of the Manyuki diet are milk and blood from our cattle, and soups derived from wild collected herbs. We boil elephant dung and drink the water. Berries and other wild fruits supplement our diet. Herbal knowledge is widespread in our community."

"Hardwoods such as this umbrella acacia are used to produce weapons. Weapons also still serve an important role in protection from wild animals."

It was at this stage that Sarah needed to excuse herself to go to the toilet. The only place was a very small little bush approximately 100 meters away.

"Please may you folks excuse me, but I need to go to the ladies room". Sarah was very self-conscious as she was the only female on the game drive.

The three men looked the other way as Sarah went to do her business.

After about five minutes, Sarah came running back to the group, short of breath, looking ashen and excited.

The three men looked at her, awaiting her to speak.

"There are human skeletal remains underneath that bush!"

CHAPTER 43:

CO-MINGLED SKELETAL REMAINS

When it came to tracking and bush interpretation, Timothy was the best of the best, which is why he was hired to be chief tracker at the prestigious *King Makohani Mountain-top lodge.*

Timothy immediately went to investigate the scene. He had some military training prior to becoming a field ranger and tracker. He didn't go to school and was trained in the bushveld. *'School slows you down'* is was what he was taught by his Manyuki teachers. To track and work in the bushveld as a tracker or in anti-poaching requires you to have been raised in the bushveld. *'One can't study the bushveld in textbooks'*, was another lesson he was taught. He scoured the area, and after a short while returned to the group.

At first he spoke with Roebuck in their native Manyuki language, which made Sarah and her dad feel a little uncomfortable.

However, shortly thereafter, Roebuck said that in the space of a couple of minutes, Timothy had been able to answer the following main questions: Were they bones? Were they human bones? What was the sex? What was the stature? What was the race? What was the age? How long have they been dead? And what was the cause of death?

Sarah looked at her dad, astounded! It would have taken a qualified forensic anthropologist several weeks, if not months, to answer those questions! Sarah's dad was also completely astounded and astonished by this! By just examining the scene, Timothy's advanced tracking knowledge and keen eye for detail - He could already answer the main questions within a short period of time. 'These African trackers are amazing!' Thought Sarah

'It looks like two adult skeletons', began Timothy.

The dating of skeletal remains – Recent bones have soft tissue adhering in the form of tendon and ligament tags, especially around the joint ends. Periosteum may be visible as fibrous material closely adherent to the shaft surface. Cartilage may also be present on articular surfaces. Animal predators may remove all soft tissue and cartilage. The density and feel of the bone, for a period a bone may be heavy and feel slightly greasy to the fingers, which may last for years. These bones were fragile and brittle, indicating old bones. Timothy estimated them to be very old bones.

'It looks like the bones of two African males. The one is middle-aged, the other is younger, perhaps a teenager. It does not look like they sustained sharp force trauma or blunt force trauma. The bones show no signs of that. There were no signs of bullets. There were no signs of fire. There are some post mortem predator injuries, probably caused by some of the animals in the Mara. But to me it looks like these two men died suddenly and at the same time.'

Timothy had found a leather ligature on the scene and he also found a broken-off distal tip of an arrow, which he held in his hand. The arrow tip looked very sharp and obviously the time and the weather had had no effect on blunting its sharpness.

It was impossible for Timothy to determine what they had specifically died from, and they would have to alert the Kenyan Police and the Kenyan Forensics Department when they got back to camp.

Timothy handed the broken-off distal tip of the arrow to Roebuck. They had a policy that if they found any weapons or artefacts in the bush, that they were to ensure that these items were reported and safely removed by the authorities.

As Roebuck took the arrow head from Timothy, the sharp edge of the blade lightly scratched the skin on his palm...

'Ow! *You pricked* me!' exclaimed Roebuck, admonishing Timothy.

'Sorry, *I didn't do that on purpose,*' responded Timothy.

Seconds later, their chief safari guide - their authoritative-, their friendly-, their knowledgeable- Roebuck - was dead...

CHAPTER 44:

THE MANAGERIAL SKILLS OF ROWAN MADOCK

What had started off as a romantic early morning African safari – had evolved into an unexpected tragedy! Things had taken an unexpected turn for the worse.

"What happened to Roebuck must surely have happened to Professor Sutcliffe and Raj Makurai!" Sarah immediately put two-and-two together! *"The arrow-tip must have been coated with the same substance as the butterfly! Sarah wondered if the two, co-mingled skeletal remains could also have been killed by this self-same butterfly poison?"*

Timothy had quickly cleaned up the table and the breakfast. Timothy and Norman immediately hoisted the dead body of Roebuck into the back of the open-top game viewing vehicle.

All three were quiet as they sped back to King Makohani mountain top Lodge. All three of them lost in their own worlds!

Sarah's dad held his daughter's hand tightly and said nothing. The car bounced along the gravel roads. Roebuck was covered with a blanket on the back seat. Norman and Sarah gazed expressionlessly into the horizon. Their combined emotions were too much for any of them to handle. They were all done.

Already waiting for them at the lodge was Rowan Madock. Timothy had radioed ahead of time and he was already briefed about the incident. Rowan stood waiting at the gate. He seemed calm and in control. He ordered his staff to help unload the body of Roebuck off the vehicle and take it to the staff quarters. Norman and Sarah were ushered to the reception and told to wait there and have a drink. However they refused. They felt partly responsible and they wanted to stay and help in any way they could.

Rowan pulled Timothy aside and briefly, quietly and professionally got the history out of him. The arrow-tip was located on the front seat. It was eyed by some of the staff members. The staff members were talking with some animation and there was a lot of commotion in the background. Rowan could sense something was happening. He asked Timothy to find out from his staff what the problem was.

Minutes later Timothy returned: *"The staff and I are all members of the Manyuki tribe. This arrow tip, we believe, is part of our cultural history. It is deeply symbolic for the Manyuki people and has been missing for over one hundred years! It is a sacred item, revered by our entire kingdom. It was this arrow tip which defeated the late King Makohani. The arrow tip is a shrine to our democracy and represents to us the end of dictatorship. Once a year this arrow tip was paraded around our entire kingdom as a reminder of our communal history."*

Rowan looked at Norman. Norman looked at Sarah. They were all speechless!

"I think we need to lock this arrow tip the Lodge safe and we need to telephone the Kenyan Police." Rowan said to all those present.

However Timothy rejected this idea.

"We need to present this arrow tip to our Chief. He will know what to do with this."

Norman calmly interrupted everyone by saying that this arrow tip was a weapon which was involved in the death of their chief guide, Roebuck and that it would be

123

important for the police to see the weapon which inflicted the death.

At this, Rowan once again took centre stage.

"We understand that this arrow tip may have cultural and traditional significance and we respect this. However, we cannot deny the fact that it killed Roebuck. Therefore we will have to disclose this to the Kenyan authorities, after which, I am sure, the arrow will be handed safely to your Chief."

His message seemed to calm the staff members and Rowan carefully took the arrow-tip off the front seat of the car. He carefully wrapped it in cloth and said that he would put it in the lodge safe until such time as the Kenyan Police arrived. In the meantime, he didn't want the scandal of this death to destroy the reputation of his dad, Sir Arthur Madock's five star resorts all over the world. He had to do damage control. He also had other guests to worry about. Some of the guests were already present and were already witnessing this spectacle.

Roebuck's body was wrapped in a blanket and taken to the staff quarters. Sarah and her dad felt shattered by this incident. Sarah and her dad still had several more days in Kenya, at this lodge, and already Sarah wanted nothing more than to go home!

That afternoon Sarah's dad planted himself at the bar and ordered a double shot of whiskey. Sarah did not usually drink alcohol, although she ordered herself a cider. On the horizon, another storm was brewing. This time it looked more ominous and threatening than the previous night. The grasslands were dry. It was incredibly hot. The animals were stressed. The lodge staff and the lodge guests were also stressed.

It turned out to be a long day. No-one felt like going on another game-drive. The guests just sat at the pool, drinking and talking. The holiday mood was ruined.

"The police will be here first thing tomorrow morning" Rowan came to tell the guests.

CHAPTER 45:

AGAIN WITHOUT A TRACE!

The following morning the Kenyan police arrived. Three large detectives drove slowly up the mountain in their marked vehicle. Rowan pointed out the body of Roebuck to the three detectives and then hovered nervously in the background.

Statements were given by Timothy, Norman and Sarah.

The other guests tried to continue as normal as possible with their holiday and sat at their breakfast tables. The mood was still low and hung over the camp like a cloud.

Come time to open the safe and show the arrow-tip to the Police – Everyone was shocked and surprised to find that it had disappeared. Despite it being in the safe! There was complete disbelief!

"The arrow-tip has disappeared!" exclaimed Rowan to all the Police.

"I swear I personally put it in the safe last night! Who could have taken it?"

Everyone looked at everyone. Everyone's eyes searched everyone's eyes. Timothy looked at Rowan angrily!

"I told you to hand the arrow-tip to our Chief for safe-keeping!" Timothy admonished Rowan

On the horizon, a small speck of dust could be seen racing toward the horizon...

'Give me your binoculars!' ordered Sarah to her dad.

"It's Patrick!"

"No it's not me!" Patrick emerged from the back of the crowd looking somewhat insulted. *"Someone has stolen my vehicle!"*

"I'm sorry Patrick! It was an honest mistake! Someone was now racing away in your 4 x 4 land-cruiser!"

"It's obviously one of the guests then!" Please get me a list of the guest names!" Rowan ordered Timothy.

CHAPTER 46:

THE NEFARIOUS DEALINGS OF FAIZEL ISHMAEL MNAMELA

Faizel Ishmael Mnamela was one of Africa's most-wanted men, according to Interpol and was on the top ten of FBI's most-wanted list. He had a long and illustrious criminal career.

He was a child soldier in Mozambique and at the age of 17, illegally walked across the border to South Africa. He walked alone, at night, crossing the Kruger National Park, braving wild animals and harsh climate. He settled in Soweto near Johannesburg where he eventually became the head of the 'Mozambique syndicate'.

At first he specialised in routine house robberies and hijackings. He then moved into the more lucrative rhino poaching trade, where the going rate for rhino horn was over R 50 000 - 00 per kilogram. His syndicate operated in all the main National Parks is South Africa.

He was now scoping out the rhino situation in Kenya. His personal net-worth was estimated to be in the order of several millions of dollars.

Faizel was staying alone at the Mountain lodge when he overheard the conversation about the arrow-tip.

"This would be the perfect weapon to assassinate an African leader or even kill a rhinocerous!" These were the first thoughts which crossed his mind.

All he had to do was get to Nairobi, board a plane, a train or a bus and head straight back to South Africa!

A quick Google search showed what a dangerous character Faizel Ishmael Mnamela was! He was also wanted for rape, murder and kidnapping. He obviously had no social conscience and was very dangerous. To think that Sarah and her dad ate dinner the previous night in the presence of this monster, who was sitting only two tables away. Granted, he was immaculately dressed at the time. His clothing hid multiple gang-related tattoos. His body also had scars from previous stab wounds and gunshot wounds.

The three Kenyan policemen were in hot pursuit of the vehicle on the horizon, which seemed to have a thirty minute lead on them. Rowan, Timothy, Norman and Sarah also followed behind them, driving slower in their own 4 x 4 land-cruiser. The chase took place on the Mara planes. It was dusty and dry and all the cars kicked up dust, making it easy for the guests on the mountain lodge to observe the chase.

Nairobi was six hours away and it looked like the cars weren't catching up with one another. The nearest town, Narok, was only about three hours away.

'Surely there must be police road blocks in Narok?'

"I am sure the three policemen will radio this in to Narok!"

Timothy was driving. Rowan was in the passenger seat. Sarah and her dad were in the back seats.

CHAPTER 47:

NAROK

Faizel Ishmael Mnamela stopped the 4 x 4 land-cruiser in the marketplace of Narok. There were thousands of people. There was loud noise. There were strange and exotic smells and odours. He could easily disappear within this chaos. He could disappear within minutes. This was his game.

The three policemen stopped their car behind the stolen 4 x 4 land-cruiser. They saw Faizel slip towards the crowds. Rowan, Timothy, Norman and Sarah stopped their 4 x 4 land-cruiser behind the police vehicle.

Faizel suddenly pulled a handgun out from under his shirt. Despite there being crowds of multiple innocent civilians, he fired three shots in the direction of the vehicles. Everyone ducked behind their cars. They could see that Faizel was going to enter the market place. He and the 'spear-tip' would soon be lost forever!

Faizel gave them a charming smile, he waved at them and gave a mock salute. He then turned to run towards the marketplace and its swathe of humanity.

Some call it luck. Others call it fate. Some call it chance. Be that as it may, serendipity always seems to play a role in all of life's events.

From the background emerges a large black woman who says nothing.

She looks familiar. Her face expressionless. It's a large, mute, African woman.

Could it be? From Kamiti prison?

She approaches the man with the gun and hugs him very tight from behind. Very tight! She won't let him go. The man suddenly becomes completely passive. He doesn't resist. He doesn't fight. His gun drops to the ground. He allows himself to be held by this large woman. They both fall to the ground like a sack of potatoes.

When the three policemen finally arrive, Faizel is completely invisible at first. The large black woman lies over him, completely engulfing his body, smothering him. Only his face is exposed, eyes wide open, trying to breathe and gasp for air. His mouth is next to his captor's ear.

The large male Kenyan police official approaches them, baton in hand.

Rowan, Timothy, Norman and Sarah also approach from behind.

And one of the policemen screams at the large African Woman.

'Let him go Mampi!'

The End